Hiya . . .

always work out the way you im
for the wrong boy . . . who might
boy, after all.

   Where does the cake come in? Well, I guess cake has
been a pretty big inspiration of mine over the years too, so
why not? I hope you enjoy *Angel Cake* - and remember: life
is sweet!

Cathy Cassidy

Books by Cathy Cassidy

DIZZY
DRIFTWOOD
INDIGO BLUE
SCARLETT
SUNDAE GIRL
LUCKY STAR
GINGERSNAPS
ANGEL CAKE

CHOCOLATE BOX GIRLS: CHERRY CRUSH

DREAMS & DOODLES DAYBOOK
LETTERS TO CATHY

For Younger Readers

SHINE ON, DAIZY STAR
DAIZY STAR AND THE PINK GUITAR
STRIKE A POSE, DAIZY STAR

Cathy Cassidy

Angel Cake

PUFFIN

PUFFIN BOOKS

Published by the Penguin Group
Penguin Books Ltd, 80 Strand, London WC2R ORL, England
Penguin Group (USA) Inc., 375 Hudson Street, New York, New York 10014, USA
Penguin Group (Canada), 90 Eglinton Avenue East, Suite 700, Toronto, Ontario, Canada M4P 2Y3
(a division of Pearson Penguin Canada Inc.)
Penguin Ireland, 25 St Stephen's Green, Dublin 2, Ireland (a division of Penguin Books Ltd)
Penguin Group (Australia), 250 Camberwell Road, Camberwell, Victoria 3124, Australia
(a division of Pearson Australia Group Pty Ltd)
Penguin Books India Pvt Ltd, 11 Community Centre, Panchsheel Park, New Delhi – 110 017, India
Penguin Group (NZ), 67 Apollo Drive, Rosedale, Auckland 0632, New Zealand
(a division of Pearson New Zealand Ltd)
Penguin Books (South Africa) (Pty) Ltd, 24 Sturdee Avenue, Rosebank, Johannesburg 2196, South Africa

Penguin Books Ltd, Registered Offices: 80 Strand, London WC2R ORL, England

puffinbooks.com

First published 2009
Published in this edition 2011
003 – 10 9 8 7 6 5 4 3

Text copyright © Cathy Cassidy, 2009
Illustrations copyright © Sara Flavell, 2009
All rights reserved

The moral right of the author and illustrator has been asserted

Set in Baskerville MT
Printed in Great Britain by Clays Ltd, St Ives plc

British Library Cataloguing in Publication Data
A CIP catalogue record for this book is available from the British Library

ISBN: 978-0-141-33890-3

www.greenpenguin.co.uk

MIX
Paper from
responsible sources
FSC
www.fsc.org   FSC™ C018179

Penguin Books is committed to a sustainable
future for our business, our readers and our
planet. This book is made from paper certified
by the Forest Stewardship Council.

Thanks . . .

To my lovely, patient husband, Liam, and my fab kids, Calum and Caitlin, for endless hugs, and also to Mum, Joan, Andy, Lori and all my family far and wide. Hugs to all my brilliant friends: Sheena, Helen, Fiona, Mary-Jane, Magi, Zarah, Jessie and the whole crew for keeping me sane . . . well, almost. Thanks to Catriona for helping with the website, organizing my life and being generally all-round fab; to Martyn for looking after the adding-up bits; and to Darley and his angels at the agency for . . . well, everything! Thanks to Amanda, the world's sweetest, smartest and most patient editor; and to Sara, the world's best cover-artist/illustrator; also to Adele, Francesca, Emily, Sophie, Sara, Kirsten, Tania, Sarah, Jennie and the whole Puffin team.

Special thanks to Ana, who started me dreaming and inspired the story, and to Polish girls Agatha, Klaudia and Kasia for helping with research; also to Andrew B. and Zosia for the same; and to Scratchy for the pyjamas-in-the-park story; and Sinead for the angel-boy one! Thanks to the two best cafes in the universe, for their inspiration and help with the cake research . . . Designs in Castle Douglas and Kitty's Tearoom in New Galloway, which actually has a cake called Angel's Wings . . . sigh.

Finally, thanks to my brilliant readers, whose feedback, support and enthusiasm make all the hard work worthwhile. You're the best!

The last few bits and pieces are packed. Mum is running around the flat with a duster, trying to make it all perfect for the next tenants, and Kazia's sitting on her suitcase hugging the old rabbit Gran knitted for her and trying not to cry.

I know how she feels. I'm excited about moving, but scared as well. I've tried so many times to picture this day, but now that it's finally here I feel numb, shaky. My stomach is full of butterflies, some of them in hobnailed boots.

Gran and Grandad arrive to take us to the airport, and then it all moves too fast. The worst bit is saying goodbye. Gran and Grandad hug me so hard it feels like they are trying to memorize the shape of me in their arms, and both of them are crying fat, salty tears even while they are telling us to be brave, to think of the future, to make the most of the new life that's waiting for us in Liverpool.

'We'll write, and phone, and email,' I promise.

'And we'll visit, and you can come over at Christmas and visit us . . .'

'Of course,' Gran says, but I know they won't. They will be with Uncle Zarek and Aunt Petra and the cousins this Christmas, in their big flat with the log fire crackling and the festive table always set with an extra place in case a lonely traveller should come knocking at the door.

By the time we get through security, Mum is crying too, and Kazia, and even I have to take a deep breath in and wipe the tears away. It is hard to leave Krakow, to leave Poland, and step into the unknown. It is hard to leave my family, my friends, the place I once called home.

It's hard, but it's what I've dreamt of too, for years.

Dad went away to work in Britain when I was nine. He could earn better money there, Mum explained, and one day, maybe soon, he would send for us. In Britain, we would have a better life. I didn't know I needed a better life, back then. The one I had seemed good enough, until Dad went away.

I missed him. I'd sit by my bedroom window, looking out beyond the city rooftops to the big, blue sky where the swallows that nested in the eaves just above our apartment swooped and soared in the late summer sun. I wondered if there were swallows in Britain, if Dad could look up, as I did, and see them dip and glide through the blue.

I wished I could fly south for the winter, like the swallows, to a place where the sun always shone. I wished we could all be together again.

In Krakow, the winters are cold – thick snow lies on the ground for months at a time. The rooftops are dusted with white sugar-frosting, and you have to wear two pairs of socks inside your boots just to stop your toes from turning blue.

'Does it snow in Britain?' my little sister, Kazia, wanted to know, when Dad came home that first Christmas.

'Sometimes,' he told us. 'But it's not as cold as Krakow!'

'Can we go back with you?' I asked.

Dad smiled. 'One day, Anya! Britain is a land of opportunity, a place where hard work is rewarded. The streets are paved with gold. Not real gold, of course, but you know what I mean.'

I kind of did. I imagined a place where everything was beautiful, where everyone smiled because they could have whatever they wanted.

'We could have a future there,' Dad said softly, his eyes bright with dreams of his own.

'Are there swallows?' I asked Dad, and he just laughed.

'Yes, there are swallows,' he said. 'Just like the

ones in Krakow. Britain is not so different, really, Anya.'

But I knew it was a world away.

It took three years for Dad to settle enough to bring us over to England, three years of postcards and letters and long-distance phone calls. Sometimes, if we were really lucky, there were little wooden toys, animals mostly, that he'd carved and painted on the long, lonely nights in England, just for Kazia and me.

Dad had to take whatever work he could find, picking fruit, on a building site, night shifts in a pickle factory. I wasn't sure how any of that could be better than his job in Krakow, managing a team of joiners and woodworkers for a big firm in town, but I didn't argue.

Then Dad came to Liverpool and met Yuri, a Ukrainian guy running an agency that placed migrant workers in jobs all over the city. Dad went into the office looking for a job and ended up as a partner in the business.

'Yuri wants to use my management experience,' Dad told us over the phone. 'And my language skills, of course. I can bring many Polish workers to the agency. With my skills, the business can grow, become the best of its kind in the north-west.'

'Wonderful,' Mum had said, but her eyes were

4

anxious. I could see that living in Britain was Dad's dream and mine, not hers, but she didn't argue.

'This is our chance,' Dad explained. 'This business will make a fortune for us. This is the start of our new life!'

Dad said he had a house for us, in a nice area, with a garden. I imagined a pretty cottage with whitewashed walls and a glossy red door and climbing roses clinging to the walls, like pictures in the books Dad used to send to help me with my English.

I imagined a new school, where the pupils wore neat uniforms and played hockey or quidditch and had midnight feasts. I imagined new friends, a boyfriend maybe.

Mum gave up her job at the bakery in town, where she had been in charge of making wedding cakes and birthday cakes and the rich, dark poppy-seed cake everyone loved to eat at Christmas. 'No more cake,' my little sister Kazia frowned.

'There will always be cake,' Mum promised. 'Life would be dull without a little sweetness now and then.'

We packed up our possessions, said our goodbyes.

And now we are on the plane, which is scary and exciting and wonderful all at the same time. None of us have ever been on a plane before, and Kazia looks scared as Mum buckles her seat belt. She hugs her knitted rabbit tightly. We are leaving our old lives behind, building new ones from scratch, in a city called Liverpool where the streets are paved with gold.

I bite my lip. The plane climbs through grey cloud, finally emerging into clear blue skies and sunshine. The clouds are far beneath us now, a carpet of soft white candyfloss. Everything feels fresh and new. It's like being on the edge of something wonderful, something you've dreamed of for years and years but never quite had within grasp until now.

Britain, at last.

I am ready for this. I have worked so hard on my English – in my last school test I came top of the class. Beside me, Kazia slips her small hand into mine. 'I won't know what to say to anyone,' she whispers. 'I can't remember any English words. It's all right for you, you're good at English!'

'So are you,' I tell my little sister. 'We'll be fine!'

'It won't be as easy outside the classroom,' Mum reminds us. 'There are accents to unravel, and your dad says Liverpool has quite a strong one. But we will settle in, I know.'

I smile and lean back against the window. I think about the swallows, making their long journey south, year after year, never knowing just what they will find. I try to be brave, like them.

We can't stay above the candyfloss clouds forever, of course, and eventually the plane begins its descent towards Liverpool John Lennon Airport. The three of us hold hands as the plane lands, our eyes wide, our hearts thumping. Climbing down the plane steps on to British soil, we find ourselves in a dark, grey world where the wind whips our hair against our faces and the rain slants down in sheets.

'Just like Krakow,' Mum jokes.

We collect our cases and go through passport control and immigration, and then we are at the gates, and Dad is there, waving madly, his face breaking into the widest grin I have ever seen.

'My girls!' he yells. 'My beautiful girls!'

We fall into his arms.

Mr. Yip's FISH EMPORIUM

Nothing about Britain is the way I thought it would be. Instead of blue skies and sunshine, there are grey clouds and endless rain that seeps into your bones, your soul. It's October, and there are no swallows, just noisy pigeons and squawking seagulls.

It's funny how quickly a dream can crumble.

The house Dad promised turns out to be a poky flat above a chippy called Mr Yip's Fish Emporium. The faded wallpaper curls away from damp walls and the smell of stale chip fat clings to everything. Dad has fixed the broken window, mended the kitchen cupboard, but still, it's a dump. There are no roses around the door, just yellow weeds between the broken paving stones and a litter of scrunched-up chip papers.

It turns out that Dad's new business isn't making his fortune after all. Instead, it's eating up most of his time and quite a bit of his savings.

'It's just a little cash-flow problem,' he explains. 'I promised you a proper house, and we will get one, definitely, once the agency is doing well. This flat – this area – is just temporary.'

Mum looks around the flat as if she might cry.

'The agency *will* take off,' Dad promises. 'You have to trust me on this. We've had a few problems, but with the cash I've been able to put into the business, we will soon be in profit. I didn't want you to change your plans – I wanted us all to be together. We've waited so long to be a family again.'

Dad puts his arms round Mum and me and Kazia, and for a moment the nightmare flat fades. We are together again. That's what matters, isn't it? And this is an adventure . . .

That's what I tell myself, curled up in a creaky bed with the moonlight flooding through stringy curtains and the sound of my little sister Kazia crying quietly into her pillow.

That's what I tell myself the next day, as we walk into town to go to Polish Mass at the Catholic cathedral. Mum, Kazia and I look around at the tall Victorian houses, which look like they've seen better days, the ragged pair of boxer shorts hanging from a tree like a flag, the beer cans in the gutter.

Even the cathedral is a disappointment. It's like a giant ice-cream cone dumped down on to the pavement, or a shiny spaceship that has landed by accident and can't quite get away again. It's a million miles from the tall, elegant churches of Krakow.

Inside, though, light streams through the stained glass. It's like being inside a giant kaleidoscope, with patches of jewel-bright colour everywhere. I listen to the Mass, close my eyes and pray for a miracle, something to rescue us from the sad and scruffy flat, the endless grey drizzle. I want my dream back, because it was way better than the reality.

After Mass, we stand on the cathedral steps while Dad introduces us to his friends and workmates.

'This is Tomasz and Stefan, who work with me,' he says, beaming. 'This is Mr and Mrs Nowak, and Mr and Mrs Zamoyski . . .'

'Pleased to meet you . . . of course, this is a difficult time to be starting out . . . there's not quite as much work in the city as there once was, but I'm sure you will be fine! Welcome, welcome!'

We shake hands and smile until our faces hurt.

'You'll find it very different from home,' one girl tells me. 'I hated it, at first.'

'Just don't show them you're scared,' another tells me.

'I'm not scared!' I argue, and the girls just look at me, smiling, as if they know better. Well, maybe they do.

The next day, I pull on a white shirt and black skirt, ready for school. I slip on a second-hand blazer, black with red piping, two sizes too big for me. It belonged to the teenage son of one of Dad's workers, who went to the same school I will be going to. He doesn't need his blazer now, because the whole family packed up and went back to Warsaw.

I look out at the grey rain, and I almost envy them.

Mum walks us to school, her lips set into a firm, determined line. The playground of St Peter and Paul's is quiet as we walk over to the office, with just a few kids in blazers hanging around in little groups.

In the office, we fill in forms, slowly, with lots of sign language and mime to help us along. Mum keeps looking at me to help explain what the office staff are saying, but it doesn't sound anything like the language I've been studying so hard at school in Krakow. It makes no sense to me at all.

The head teacher, Mr Fisher, shakes my hand and tells me, very loudly and very slowly, that he hopes I will be happy here. And then Mum and Kazia are gone, to go through the whole thing again at Kazia's new primary school, and I am left alone.

When I step out into the corridor this time, there is a sea of teenagers, pushing, shoving, laughing, yelling. A school secretary leads the way, bulldozing through the crowd to deliver me to Room 21a. She ushers me inside and disappears back to her office, and kids descend on me like crows picking over a roadkill rabbit.

They prod, they poke, they tug at the sleeve of

my too-big blazer, and all the time they are talking, laughing, asking questions. I can't understand anything at all. By the time the teacher turns up, the questions have got louder, slower, with accompanying sighs and rolling of eyes.

'WHAT . . . IS . . . YOUR . . . NAME?'

'WHERE . . . DO . . . YOU . . . COME . . . FROM?'

I open my mouth to answer, but my voice has deserted me, and the teacher raps on her desk for silence. I slump into a front-row seat, shaken, my eyes suddenly brimming with tears.

I remember what the Polish girls said, at Mass yesterday, and try to look brave. On the way to my next class, a couple of kids adopt me, dragging me from classroom to lunch hall like a stray dog on a bit of string.

'This is Anya,' they tell everyone. 'She's from POLAND! Go on, say something, Anya!'

Every time I open my mouth, people laugh and roll their eyes. 'What?' they yell. 'Don't they have schools, where you come from? Stick with me, I'll look after you . . .'

I am a novelty, a joke. By the end of the day, I am exhausted. I am so far out of my depth I don't know how I'll find the courage to ever return. This school is nothing like the ones in the English books Dad used to send me, nothing at all.

I will never fit in here, not in a million years.

When I get home to the poky flat above the chippy, my little sister Kazia is dancing around the living room, singing a song she has learnt in English. She runs up to me, waving a reading book at me.

'I made three new friends today!' she tells me. 'Jodie, Lauren and Amber. My teacher is called Miss Green. She's really nice! How was your school?'

'Fine,' I tell her, through gritted teeth.

'I like it here,' Kazia decides. 'Everyone is really friendly.'

I can't be jealous because my little sister is settling in so easily . . . can I?

'And guess what?' Mum chips in. 'I've found myself a job, so I can help your dad out with the cash flow, and hopefully get us out of this place and into somewhere a bit . . . well, nicer.'

'Right,' I say. 'What's the job?'

Mum looks shifty. 'It's just cleaning work, actually,' she admits. 'My English isn't good, so I couldn't expect much more. Still, I've never been afraid of a bit of elbow grease. It's a start.'

I try for a smile, but it's a struggle. 'Mum?' I ask in a quiet voice. 'What happens if we try and try, and just don't settle in? If we decide we don't like it here? What if Britain is not for us?'

Mum frowns. 'We will settle, Anya,' she tells me firmly. 'I know the flat is not what we expected, and that school will be hard for you at first. It was always going to be difficult, but we have opportunities here, a chance for a better future. Your dad has worked so hard for this . . . we must make it work. There's no going back.'

No going back. I think of the sunlight glinting on the River Wisla, the swallows swooping, crisp white snow on the rooftops, of my best friend Nadia sitting alone next to an empty desk that used to be mine.

My heart feels cold and heavy, like a stone inside my chest.

Two weeks later, I'm still praying for a miracle. You don't really get miracles at St Peter and Paul's, though, just grey-faced teachers and chaotic kids and lessons that make no sense at all.

It's not so much a school as a zoo. The pupils are like wild animals, pushing, shoving, yelling, squealing. They stared at me with curiosity those first few days, like I was a new exhibit, and I guess that's just what I was.

I thought I was good at English, but I was wrong. At first I knew nothing, understood nothing. Words swirled around me like a snowstorm, numbing my head and making my ears ache.

I've tuned in to the accent now, but it's too late. The kids have lost interest, moved on. They leave me alone, mostly. I've given up on trying to communicate – staying silent is safer. Pity I can't be invisible too. I am tired of teachers who sigh and shake their heads, of kids who wave their hands about in frantic sign language or turn up the volume and yell when I don't understand them the first time.

It's better to keep my mouth shut. The teachers forget about me and the kids talk about me as if I am deaf as well as silent. Sometimes, I wish I was.

'It must be tough, coming to a new country where you don't understand the language. I feel sorry for her . . .'

'You'd think she'd try, though. What's she doing here if she doesn't even want to learn the language? My dad says these Eastern Europeans come over here and take all the best jobs and houses . . .'

'Most of them are on benefits. They don't *want* to work . . .'

'She looks terrified. Does she think we're going to eat her?'

'Well, she looks good enough to eat . . . hey, Blondie, sit by me, I'll give you some English lessons!'

I think it was better when I didn't understand.

In PSE, the kids chuck paper planes about when the teacher's back is turned. PSE is short for Personal and Social Education. At first I didn't understand why anyone would need lessons in how to be a balanced and sociable person, but after two weeks at St Peter and Paul's I am beginning to see. The kids here need all the help they can get.

They roll their eyes and pass notes to each other

while the teacher talks about coping with difficult feelings. Nobody is listening.

Miss Matthews is young, keen, smiley. In Krakow, the kids would have loved her, but here they read magazines beneath the desk and whisper about last night's episode of *Hollyoaks*. Lily Caldwell is painting her nails under the desk, a glittery purple colour that matches her eyeshadow.

Miss Matthews writes up a title on the whiteboard: *The Worst Day of My Life*. She asks us to draw on our emotions and experiences, to write from the heart.

I could choose any day from the last two weeks, any day at all.

So far, I haven't even tried to take part in the lessons. There is a support teacher in some classes, but she doesn't speak Polish so she's not much help. She gives me worksheets with line drawings of farmyard animals and food and clothes, along with the words in English. You have to match the words with the pictures. Fun, right?

Mostly, I sit silently, dreaming of Krakow summer skies. At the end of each lesson, I copy down the homework, close my book and forget it. How can I learn chemistry and history when I barely know the language? Why attempt French when I can't even work out English? I have tried a little in Maths and art, where words don't matter as much, but even there I haven't a clue if I'm doing the right thing.

Trying to take part in PSE would be just plain crazy – my vocabulary is small, my grammar worse than useless. It would be asking for trouble. *The Worst Day of my Life* . . .

Somehow my exercise book is open. My pen moves over a clean, white page. Words pour out, words about my first day here, about hopes and dreams turning to dust in the grey corridors, about cold-eyed teachers, kids circling round like packs of wild dogs who might tear you apart at any minute . . .

Miss Matthews raps on the desk to catch our attention, and I snap my exercise book shut.

'Thank you, 8x,' she says brightly. 'Is there anyone who would like to share their work with the class?'

The silence is deafening. I could have told her that – write from the heart and then read it out loud? Er, no. Most kids would rather have their teeth pulled, without anaesthetic.

'Let's not be shy. Who'll go first?'

Lily Caldwell yawns and closes her exercise book.

Miss Matthews looks nervous. 'Frances? Kurt?' she asks hopefully. 'Chantel?'

Silence.

She won't ask me, I know – teachers never ask me anything. If they see me writing, they assume I am filling out my language worksheets or doodling in the margins. Just as well. How would the kids here feel if they know I have described them as wild animals?

'Dan, perhaps?'

Dan is a tall, mixed-race boy sitting across the aisle from me. He has melted chocolate eyes and slanting cheekbones and skin the colour of caramel. He has ink-black hair twisted into tiny braids that stick up from his head and droop over his forehead. Just one thing stops Dan from being cute – his mouth, which is curled into a scowl.

'No chance,' Dan says.

Miss Matthews looks desperate. 'Someone has to start, Dan,' she says. 'Please? I noticed that you wrote quite a lot . . .'

Dan sighs. He picks up his exercise book and tears it in half, then in half again, and again, until he has a heap of confetti on the desk in front of him.

I'd say it's pretty clear that he does not want to read out loud.

'Daniel!' Miss Matthews yelps. 'You can't – you mustn't – that book is school property!'

Dan raises an eyebrow. He doesn't seem too worried. I watch, horrified, as Lily leans across and passes him a plastic lighter under the desk. Dan flicks the lighter a few times, then touches the flame to the little pile of exercise-book confetti. With one curl of smoke, it becomes a desktop bonfire.

Dan pulls on his rucksack and saunters out of the door without a backward glance.

The class is in uproar. Girls are screaming, boys are laughing, and everyone is on their feet, trying to get a safe distance from the flames. Miss Matthews looks as if she might cry. She wrenches a fire extinguisher off the wall and sprays the mini bonfire with a mountain of white foam.

Maybe I was wrong with the whole wild animals thing. This is not a zoo, it's more of a prison riot.

'I think it's out!' Miss Matthews announces, peering at the foam-soaked desk. 'Panic over, children. You can all go back to your seats!'

That's when the fire alarm starts to screech.

Worst day ever? For Miss Matthews, this is probably it.

'Walk quietly now!' Miss Matthews pleads. 'No need to take your bags . . .' Everyone takes them anyway. The class bursts into the corridor, stampedes towards the stairs. Kids spill out from neighbouring classrooms and I am carried along in a sea of whooping teenagers, elbowing their way to freedom.

We line up in our tutor groups on the grass at the top of the playing fields, huddled together in the drizzle. Miss Matthews checks the register, frowning.

'Two missing,' she sighs. 'Dan Carney and Kurt Jones.'

It's kind of obvious why Dan has gone missing. If I were him, I'd make myself scarce too.

Kurt's absence is more worrying. He is a quiet, geeky boy with thick glasses and threadbare trousers that flap around his ankles.

'I think I saw him running towards the science block,' a plump girl called Frances McGee says. 'What if he's trapped in the flames? Fighting for his breath in all that thick, black smoke?'

'There are no flames,' snaps Lily Caldwell. 'There was hardly a fire at all, remember? I bet Dan set off the fire alarm on his way out, for a laugh.'

'But what about Kurt? Has anyone seen him?'

Lily shrugs. 'Kurt's most likely locked himself in the girls' toilets, crying. He is such a freak.'

'Enough, Lily,' Miss Matthews says. 'This is serious. If you have nothing useful to say, say nothing at all.'

Lily smirks. 'There's Mr Fisher, Miss,' she points out, as the Head approaches, his face serious. 'I bet he wants a word with you. After all, the fire started in your classroom . . . and now you've lost two of your pupils, as well!'

Miss Matthews flushes pink and turns to greet the Head, and class 8x break into little groups, chatting. I have no friends to chat with, so I lurk at a distance, hugging my satchel. That's when I see Kurt Jones, skulking along the side of the running track, behind the lines of Year Eight pupils.

He sees me watching and brings a finger up to his lips, eyes wide above the rim of his glasses, asking me to be quiet. Well, that's easy. When am I ever anything else?

Kurt sneaks closer, coming to a halt beside me.

'I don't think they've missed me,' he says. 'Have they?'

I bite my lip and nod, and Kurt's face comes to life.

'You know what I'm saying!' he says. 'Awesome!' His smile falters. 'Um . . . so, they definitely know I was missing?'

I nod again.

'Well, no worries. It's not like they can prove anything. Unless they actually catch me *with* the evidence –'

Mr Fisher's voice booms out across the grass. 'Kurt Jones! Come here this minute!'

'Oops. Speaking of evidence, I'd best get rid of it – for now, anyway. Hang on to this for me – and keep it hidden!' He pulls something out from under his blazer and stuffs it into my satchel, then strides towards Mr Fisher and Miss Matthews.

'Where've you been, Kurt?' Lily Caldwell pipes up. 'Popped out to the charity shop for those gorgeous crimplene flares, did you? You're so cool!'

Kurt ignores the jibe. The Head herds him away, and he looks back over his shoulder, eyebrows at an anxious slant. I hold my fingers to my lips, and he rewards me with a smile.

When they are out of sight, I delve into my satchel to see just what he's planted on me.

My fingers slide across books, gym kit, pencil case, then recoil in horror as they touch something warm and furry.

I blink. No . . . no way. I must have imagined it.

I reach down again, then jump back as something

23

soft and fast and panic-stricken darts away from my touch. Kurt Jones has put a small, furry animal in my satchel. I lift up the flap and peer inside, and a small, pale, pointy face with beady black eyes and a twitching nose stares back at me.

It's a rat.

The really annoying thing about Kurt Jones is that he has vanished off the face of the earth, leaving me stranded with a rat in my satchel. This is not good.

I don't even like rats – their yellow teeth and twitching whiskers make me nervous, and their tails look pink and naked. I can't help thinking of a fairy tale Mum used to tell me, about a town plagued by rats and a mysterious piper who lured first the rats and then the town's children away into the mountains. That story always made me shiver.

Still, this rat is clearly tame. It's a creamy colour, with fawn and brown patches and very bright eyes. I just can't work out what it's doing in my satchel.

By the time the fire brigade have checked over every inch of the school for smouldering exercise books, it's past midday. We trail back to Miss Matthews's classroom to collect up stray bags and hand in our folders. Dan Carney's desk is no longer heaped with flaming paper or mountains of foam, though there is a slightly charred look about it. The bell rings for lunch and I slope off to the canteen. And there is still no sign of Kurt Jones.

I think the rat is hungry, because he has eaten most of my language worksheet. It's the one about food, which is kind of appropriate. I choose a rat-friendly lunch, heaping my plate with lettuce, tomato and cheese salad.

I find a corner table and lift my satchel flap. The rat peers out, eyes glinting, whiskers twitching. I offer him a tomato, but he just sniffs and looks up at me, reproachfully. I'm tempting him with morsels of lettuce when Frances McGee slides into a seat across from me.

'Salad?' she says, frowning at my plate. 'That's rabbit food.'

Rat food, actually, but I don't say anything. Frances has a tray heaped high with pizza and chips, a can of Coke, a packet of crisps, a bar of chocolate and a large helping of apple pie and custard. She is obviously not a salad kind of girl.

I stuff a slice of cheese into my satchel and fasten the straps firmly. I am pretty sure rats are not allowed in the school canteen, not even tame ones.

'You don't say much,' Frances comments, biting into her pizza. 'Everyone thinks you're either dim or stuck up, but I reckon you're just shy. I think you're taking everything in. Are you?'

What am I supposed to say? *Yes, I'm taking it all in*

and I really, really don't like what I see? That would go down well.

'Don't you want to make friends?' she asks.

I take a long look at Frances. She's kind of strange. Her crimped and backcombed hair is dyed black and crowned with a red spotty hairband, and her lips are painted neon pink. She is wearing black net fingerless gloves, black lacy tights and clumpy boots, but nothing can disguise the fact that she's a few kilos overweight. Her school sweater looks like it would be too big for my dad, and her frilled black miniskirt only draws attention to wobbly thighs and pudgy knees.

I am not sure I really want a friend like Frances. Then again, it's not like I can afford to pick and choose, not these days. Am I going to be the kind of girl who has only a rat for a friend? It's not even my rat, either.

I look at Frances McGee and try for a smile. It's a very small smile, but Frances spots it and starts to grin.

'You can call me Frankie, if you like,' she says.

Before I can decide whether to risk saying anything, Lily Caldwell glides up to the table, her mouth twisted into a sneer.

'What's up, Frances?' she says, looking at the plump girl's tray. Her voice drips sarcasm. 'Not hungry today? On a diet? Didn't fancy the treacle pudding or the jelly and ice cream? Sure you can't fit in a plate of chicken nuggets? We don't want you wasting away, now do we?'

Frances opens her mouth to protest, then closes it again. A red stain seeps across her cheeks, and her gaze drops to the tabletop.

'Get a grip,' Lily sneers. 'You've got enough to feed the whole of Year Eight on that tray. It wouldn't hurt you to miss a meal once in a while, Frances. You could live for months on that blubber.'

Lily's hands are on her hips and her pretty face is scrunched up into a mean, pinched mask. She is telling Frances that fat girls really shouldn't wear lacy tights and miniskirts, that seeing her shovelling in the pizza is putting kids off their lunch.

I bite my lip. Sometimes, it is very, very hard to stay quiet.

'I'm only telling you this for your own good,' Lily says. 'Someone has to, right? As a friend. I'm trying to *help* you, Frances.'

I catch Lily's eye, keeping my eyes steady and my chin tilted, and give her a long, hard look. It stops Lily in her tracks.

'What are you looking at, Tanya, Anya, whatever your name is?' she snarls. 'If you've got something to say, say it!'

But I don't have the words to argue, or the confidence, or the grammar. I know I will trip over my words, tangle up their meanings, struggle with the accent, but I am angry. I'm angry for myself, after a fortnight in this dump surrounded by wild animals. I'm angry for Frances, for Kurt, for all the kids who die a little bit when Lily and others like her laugh at them, chip away at their confidence with mean words and sneering glances.

I may not have the words, but I do have something to fight back with. I undo the straps on my satchel, lift the flap.

'Oh, I forgot, you don't talk, do you?' Lily sneers. 'Face it, Sauerkraut Girl, you don't belong here . . . so why don't you just back off and mind your own business? Go back to wherever you came from . . .'

Her voice trails away into silence as the rat sprints neatly over her spike-heeled boots, then pauses, twitching, to look around.

Lily Caldwell may be a mean girl, but there is nothing wrong with her eyesight. Or her vocal chords.

'RAAAAAAAT!' she screeches, in a voice that could shatter glass.

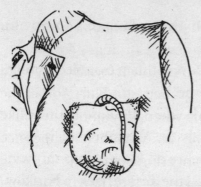

Lily, Frances and I are sitting on hard plastic chairs outside Mr Fisher's room. We are in big trouble. The little row in the canteen escalated into a full-on riot, with girls standing on tabletops, screaming, and boys skidding about trying to catch the rat.

Things got a little out of hand, with chips, doughnuts and dollops of rice pudding being flung about. One dinner lady fainted and landed face down in the fruit salad.

When Mr Fisher finally got the place in order, he looked around for the ringleaders.

'How did this start?' he roared, and all eyes swivelled to Lily, Frances and me. As he marched us out of the canteen in disgrace, I looked back over my shoulder and caught sight of Kurt Jones, sitting on the window ledge. A small, whiskery nose stuck out of his blazer pocket, sniffed politely and disappeared from view.

'This is crazy,' Lily fumes. 'How come we're

getting the blame? Like it's our fault this dump of a school is rat-infested!'

'I'm going to be in sooooo much trouble!' Frances wails. 'My mum'll kill me!'

Me, I keep a dignified silence, because I don't quite know the English words for 'Your school is like a lunatic asylum, the kids are all insane, chip-throwing arsonists and I wish I had the airfare back to Krakow.' Just as well. It might sound kind of harsh.

I'm right, though, about the lunatic asylum bit. It turns out that the three of us are not in trouble for arguing in the canteen, nor even for starting a school riot. No, it's weirder than that. We are accused of stealing a rat from the biology lab.

'What?' Lily snaps, when Mr Fisher explains the situation and asks us to tell him anything we might know, before the police are called in. 'You think I nicked that scabby rat? Yeah, right!'

'I am trying to get to the bottom of a serious crime,' Mr Fisher replies. 'The rat was taken from his cage this morning, by person or persons unknown, possibly under cover of the fire alarm. A message was scrawled on the whiteboard in the biology lab . . . *Rats have rights.*'

'Rats have what?' Lily chokes. 'Er, no. They don't have rights, they have fleas and germs and plague and horrible yellow teeth –'

'I take it you have no animal rights sympathies

then,' Mr Fisher probes, and Lily rolls her eyes and huffs as if the head teacher is an especially annoying insect she'd really like to swat.

'Animal rights?' Frances echoes. 'What do you mean? Are you saying that rat was *rescued* from the lab? What were they going to do with it? They don't dissect rats in schools any more, surely?'

'No, they don't,' Mr Fisher assures her. '*We* don't. But I fear that the misguided pupil who took the rat may have seen the whole episode as a rescue, yes . . . whereas, in fact, the rat was just Mr Critchley's pet.'

'Gross,' Lily says.

'Spooky,' Frances adds.

'And you know nothing about the theft?' he presses.

'No, Sir,' the two girls chorus.

'Anya?' Mr Fisher turns to me. 'I know you've been finding it hard to settle in here, and that you come, of course, from a very different culture. The children in the canteen reported a confrontation between you, Lily and Frances, this lunchtime. And then, very conveniently, the rat appeared, right at your feet. Anya . . . did *you* take the rat from the biology lab?'

'No, Sir,' I tell him.

But I think I know who did.

*

We end up in after-school detention, Lily, Frances and me.

When Mr Fisher abandoned his search for the rat-napper and tried to unravel the canteen bullying incident, he met with a brick wall. Lily insisted the three of us were the best of friends, Frances blinked hard and agreed there really wasn't a problem and I just sat there, stunned and silent.

Mr Fisher didn't buy the cover-up, and kept us all in after the final bell.

'I cannot help you unless you let me,' he tells us now. 'There was definitely something going on, this lunchtime. I don't know if it was bullying, or if it was linked to the missing rat, but it was definitely something. One way or another, I intend to find out!'

'Yes, Sir,' Frances says, rolling her eyes.

We sit in silence, writing out the legend *I must respect my fellow pupils* over and over again. It's a bit much, when Lily is the only one of us to have a problem with respect.

Over in the corner, Kurt Jones is writing lines too.

'He's in trouble for going missing during the fire alarm,' Frances whispers, raising an eyebrow. 'Good job Fisher hasn't worked out where he really was . . .'

I remember Frances telling Miss Matthews that

she saw Kurt running towards the science block earlier, and follow her gaze across the room. Kurt is leaning over his desk, the tip of a slim pink tail just visible, sticking out of a blazer pocket.

At four o'clock, Mr Fisher looks at his watch. 'Well, young man,' he says to Kurt Jones. 'I hope you've learnt your lesson! Disappearing during a fire alarm is a very serious matter, even if you did need to go to the toilet rather urgently. We searched high and low for you!'

'Sorry, Sir,' Kurt says. 'It won't happen again.'

'As for you girls,' Mr Fisher continues, 'I am not happy about today's little scene in the lunch hall . . . not happy at all. I will be watching you all very carefully.'

'Will you, Sir?' Lily Caldwell says, fluttering her eyelashes and sticking her chest out a little. 'Oh!'

Mr Fisher turns a startling shade of pink. 'Off you go home,' he says, exasperated. 'All of you.'

The four of us straggle out into the rain. Kurt gives us a wave and strides on ahead, his school bag swinging, his flared trousers flapping gently in the breeze. Lily Caldwell huddles in the doorway, beneath a Hello Kitty umbrella, lighting a ciggy. She is trying to look cool and hard, but coughing way too much to look either.

Frances McGee falls into step beside me. 'That girl is something else,' she says darkly as we walk up towards Aigburth Road, dodging the puddles. 'Poisonous little witch.'

'Lily is not nice girl,' I sigh.

'I was right, wasn't I?' Frances says. 'You understand a whole lot more than you let on. And you can speak, if you want to! So . . . friends?' Frances tugs down her beanie hat against the rain.

'Yes, friends,' I tell her.

'Call me Frankie,' she says, and links my arm, and the two of us walk along together. 'What a day,' she sighs. 'Arson, animal rights kidnappings, fights in the canteen, rat riots, detentions . . .'

'School in England is not like home,' I say carefully.

'Well, not every day is like today,' she laughs. 'It's not usually this good!'

I frown. I don't think I've got the hang of this English sense of humour yet.

'Does it rain always, in Liverpool?' I ask.

Frankie laughs. 'Of course not! The weather has been yucky since you arrived, I admit . . .' She looks at me, her plump face kind. 'You hate it, don't you, Anya?'

'No, I . . .' The words have deserted me, and I wipe a hand across my face, pretending I'm wiping away raindrops and not tears.

'It's not so bad,' Frankie says. 'Who knows, you might even get to like it. Miracles do happen!'

Yeah, right. Then again, I guess it's never too late to hope.

We turn the corner into Aigburth Road, and there on the pavement in front of the shops is . . . an angel.

Seriously – a dark-haired boy wearing white-feathered angel wings is standing on the kerb, facing away from us, holding a tray and a large white umbrella.

Then he turns round and I do a double take, because this is not an angel at all, it's Dan Carney. At least, I think it is.

It's hard to tell, because he isn't burning exercise books or setting off fire alarms, and he isn't scowling. He is carrying a big tray of home-made cupcakes, all pastel icing and sugar-strand sprinkles, tilting the umbrella carefully to keep them dry. His soft brown eyes are shining behind a fall of braided hair, his mouth stretched wide into a grin. Then he sees us, and his face falls.

'Do you see what I see?' Frankie says, holding my arm a little tighter.

'I see,' I tell her.

'Angel boy,' Frankie says, and it takes me a moment to realize what she means, because the Polish word for 'English' is *angielski*, which sounds an awful lot like the English word for 'angel'. Dan Carney may be English, but I'm not sure if he's an angel, even with the wings.

He looks around, as if checking for escape routes, but short of sprinting across the busy road or loitering under the awning of a shop that sells ladies' underwear, he has nowhere to go. He stands his ground, trying to hide behind the umbrella.

'He's selling cakes,' Frankie whispers. 'Must be a part-time job. C'mon, let's take a look!'

She drags me over, lifts up the white umbrella and pulls me under its shelter. We are face to face with Dan Carney, the mad arsonist of Year Eight. Up close, I'd swear I can see a faint pink blush beneath the caramel skin of his cheeks. I can smell vanilla, warm and sweet, but that's probably the cakes, of course.

'All right, Frankie?' Dan Carney says. 'Anya?'

He knows my name. I thought I was invisible, but Dan Carney can see me. His melted chocolate eyes hold mine over the tray of cakes, turning my insides to mush. Then the umbrella tilts, and a dribble of cold rain slides down the back of my neck, bringing me down to earth.

'It's funny, Dan,' Frankie is saying, tugging at one of his white-feathered wings. 'I never had you down as an angel.'

'I have hidden depths,' he says with a sigh. 'Just don't tell anyone, OK? How come you're so late out of school, anyhow? I thought I was safe. Thought everyone had gone . . .'

'Detention,' Frankie says. 'Some divvy set fire to his desk this morning, and the whole day went downhill from there . . . remind me to tell you about it, sometime.'

'Don't bother,' he says. 'It's old news. Want a cupcake?'

It turns out that Dan Carney isn't actually selling anything – he is giving away cupcakes for free. He explains that this is the opening day of a brand-new cafe, Heaven, and that as a special promotion he is giving away a free voucher for cakes and drinks to a few very special customers.

'Us?' Frankie snorts. 'What's special about us? What's the catch?'

'No catch,' Dan shrugs. 'The boss is just trying to attract the right kind of customers. People who could become regulars, tell their friends, that kind of thing.'

'Are you saying I look like the kind of person who eats a lot of cake?' Frankie bristles. 'What does that mean?'

Dan rolls his eyes. 'I'm not saying that,' he says. 'I'm just saying . . . look, this is the opening day of my mum's new cafe. It's chucking down with rain, and we need customers. And it's free, OK? Please? For me?'

'Whatever,' Frankie says, taking a cake and handing one to me. 'Why didn't you just say?'

'I thought I did,' he sighs. 'So . . . what d'you think? Good, huh?'

I take a bite and nod, smiling, as the sweet pink frosting melts on my tongue and sinks into my soul.

'Awesome!' Frankie whispers, between mouthfuls. 'Vouchers for free cake, you said? Count us in!'

Dan laughs and hands us a couple of pastel printed flyers apiece. *Heaven*, the flyer reads. *Where life is sweet.* There's an address and a snip-off voucher for the promised freebies.

'It's just across the road, in Lark Lane,' he tells us. 'Anya, you're soaking . . . haven't you even got a hat? Look, take the umbrella, OK? I can hang around under the awning.'

Definitely a miracle.

I smile shyly at Dan from behind my dripping hair, and Frankie laughs, grabbing the umbrella. 'You really are an angel, aren't you, Dan?'

'You'd better believe it,' he says.

Heaven is warm and dry, with pale squashy sofas and mismatched tables and chairs. The place is packed. A gaggle of mums with noisy toddlers tuck messily into cake, and a couple of old grannies in plastic rain hats are chatting in the corner.

And then there are the cakes . . . a whole long

counter of them, behind sparkling glass. There's a chocolate layer cake, a vast Victoria sponge, an apple and caramel pie, a mountain of glazed fruit tarts and something amazing made of strawberries, cream and fluffy meringue.

Frankie pinches herself, then me, hard.

'Ow!' I protest.

'It's real, isn't it?' she whispers. 'This place. I'm not imagining it, right? First, the school firestarter chats us up in the street and lends us his umbrella. Then he gives us free cake and sends us here!'

'It is real,' I tell her.

I take in a deep breath. I can smell baking, sweet and warm, in the background. The aroma wraps itself round me like a hug.

A smiley boy of about nine, in angel wings and a *Heaven* T-shirt, comes to greet us. His chocolate eyes and caramel skin mark him down as Dan's little brother, and I can see another, younger, boy, also in angel wings, carrying a tray of cakes to the chatting grannies.

'Have you got vouchers?' the boy asks. 'Did Dan send you?'

We nod, and he leads us through the crowded cafe. 'It's a bit crazy,' he explains. 'It's our first day, and the vouchers have been popular . . . but we have a few seats left, if you don't mind sharing?'

'We don't mind,' Frankie says.

'Just in the corner here . . .' the boy says.

Sitting at the corner table, slurping noisily on a tall strawberry milkshake, is Kurt Jones. On the table in front of him stands a tall, tiered cake rack laden with slices of sponge and gateau, cream scones, fruit slices, strawberry meringues.

'Hey,' Frankie says, sliding into a seat. 'If it isn't the mystery rat-napper!'

'Shhh,' Kurt says. 'They're very nice here, but I'm not sure Cheesy would be welcome. There are probably health and safety regulations.'

'Cheesy?' I echo.

'The rat,' Kurt explains. 'That seems to be his favourite food. I had a cheese and pickle roll in my rucksack, and he ate the whole thing in double maths.'

'Keep him hidden, or you'll get us all thrown out,' Frankie hisses. 'I want my free cake! Dan Carney in angel wings . . . what a laugh! Devil horns and a tail would be more his style. Seriously, this has been one crazy day!'

'It's not over yet,' Kurt says, and I follow his eyes. The littlest waiter is carrying a tray of milkshakes across to our table. Someone is following him.

'There's a seat here,' the boy says.

Lily Caldwell slips into an empty chair with a face that could turn milk sour.

'This sucks,' Lily says, looking around the table with a sneer. 'What are you losers doing here?'

'Nice to see you too, Lily,' Frankie says.

Lily just curls her lip. 'Dan said the vouchers were for special customers,' she huffs. 'What makes you all so special?'

'Our wit, our charm, our sparkling good looks?' Kurt quips, selecting a slice of cream sponge from the tiered cake plate. 'Oh, yeah – and we're willing to put up with you.'

'Or not,' Frankie mutters under her breath.

'Don't kid yourselves that I want to sit with you no-hopers,' Lily snarls. 'I'm only here for the free cake. Dan said he'd come and join me, once he managed to ditch the flyers and the cupcakes. Hopefully, you lot will have gone by then.'

My shoulders slump. Dan Carney may have given me a cupcake, an umbrella and a look that turned my insides to mush, but he definitely didn't make a date for later. I guess that Lily, with her sparkly eyeshadow and her acid tongue, is much more his type. Anybody would be more his type, really, than me.

Silent, drenched and miserable is not a look many boys go for.

'Pity this place doesn't do wholemeal options,' Kurt is saying. 'Sugar and cream and white flour are not good for you. What this area needs is a really good wholefood cafe. You can do amazing things with seeds and walnuts and chopped dates.'

'Get a life, freak,' Lily snaps, her eyes skimming over Kurt's lank hair, his skinny shoulders, the sagging school sweater that looks like it came from a jumble sale. 'Who wants some stodgy old cake stuffed with nuts and seeds and dried fruit?'

Lily's description sounds a lot like the cakes my mum used to make at the bakery in Krakow, and they were really popular. I'm not about to argue, though.

'This cream sponge may not be the healthiest cake on the planet,' Frankie tells Kurt. 'But it looks like the tastiest . . . go on, one slice won't hurt!'

Lily snorts. 'That's a laugh! You're the last person who needs free cake, Frances McGee,' she says. 'There must be, like, a million calories in this stuff. You'll be the size of a whale. Oh, I forgot, you already are!'

I watch Frankie's cheeks flare crimson and wish I had the courage to slap Lily Caldwell. Frankie's words *poisonous little witch* spring to mind. If nothing else, Lily is expanding my English vocabulary.

It's a pity I don't have a rat in my satchel to shut her up with this time, but Kurt comes to the rescue instead.

'Just leave it, Lily, OK?' he says.

'What?' she asks, raising an eyebrow. 'Leave what? I was just saying. As a friend.'

But Kurt stares her down, and she shrugs, takes a meringue and bites into it, and slowly the sharpness dissolves from her face and she smiles, a soft, sweet, smile.

I blink, looking round the table. Kurt sighs and closes his eyes as he bites into his cream sponge. I don't think he's worrying too much about walnuts and chopped dates now. Frankie hesitates over her slice of chocolate cake, then she caves in and tastes it. Her eyes widen, and her lips form a little 'o' of pure delight.

'What the heck do they put in this stuff?' Frankie whispers. 'I never tasted anything like it. Awesome!'

Kurt sighs. 'No wonder they call this place Heaven!'

'I suppose Dan did us all a favour,' Lily says grudgingly. 'Not just with the free cake, either. His stunt with the flaming exercise book was cool. It got us out of morning lessons, after all.'

Her face darkens as she frowns at Frankie and

me. 'And then I got out of afternoon lessons as well, thanks to you two . . . and whichever moron stole that flea-bitten rat from the biology lab.'

'Oh?' Kurt asks, all innocence.

'Didn't you hear? Someone nicked Mr Critchley's rat while the fire alarm was ringing,' Lily explains. 'Probably some animal rights nut who thought it was still legal to experiment on animals.'

'It is still legal,' Kurt says.

'Not in schools. The Head says that rat was Mr Critchley's pet,' Frankie points out.

'Maybe,' Kurt shrugs. 'Maybe not. I don't trust him. He used to keep rats in the lab and kill them so the kids could dissect them, just to show stupid, random stuff, like how long a rat's intestine is.'

'Yuck,' Frankie says. 'That's like something from the dark ages!'

'It wasn't so long ago,' Kurt says. 'My dad went to St Peter and Paul's, back in the nineties, and Mr Critchley taught him. Dad got excluded for three days, once, for refusing to cut up a rat.'

Lily pulls a face. 'Don't tell me,' she says. 'I bet your dad's some saddo hippy loser, just like you.'

Kurt blinks. 'My dad's dead,' he says quietly. 'He and my mum were killed in a car crash when I was three.'

A shiver runs down my spine, and my cake fork drops on to the tabletop with a clatter.

45

Lily is mortified. 'I'm sorry!' she whispers, her face pale. 'I didn't know, Kurt, honest . . .'

'Oh, Kurt,' Frankie echoes. 'That's just so sad!'

He shrugs. 'I was only a toddler,' he explains. 'I don't remember much about them, but I live with my gran, and she tells me stories of the things Dad used to do. I couldn't believe it when I heard the rat story. I never did like Mr Critchley, but knowing that he got my dad excluded like that –'

'The loser!' Lily says angrily. She has changed sides instantly. 'I've always said Critchley is a creep . . .'

'And he still keeps a rat in his classroom,' Frankie breathes. 'What a sicko!'

'I guess my dad *might* have been a bit like me,' Kurt is saying. 'He was the sort of person who stood up for what he believed in, and . . . well . . .'

Lily's mouth drops open. 'It was you!' she gasps. 'You stole Mr Critchley's rat!'

Kurt smiles. 'I prefer to think of it as a rescue,' he says.

'But what . . . where . . .'

'Don't worry, Lily,' Kurt assures her. 'The rat is in a safe place.'

I am glad Lily is sitting on the other side of the table, because that means she can't see the twitching pink nose that pokes out briefly from Kurt's rucksack, then disappears again.

'Hang on,' Lily argues. 'Where exactly . . .'

I chew my lip. If Lily spots the rat, things could get very nasty. A repeat performance of the canteen rat-riots is not what Heaven needs at all.

Luckily, at that moment the steamed-up cafe door swings open and Dan Carney comes in, his black hair plastered to his head, wings dripping.

'Dan!' Lily yells. 'Over here! I've been saving you a seat!'

Dan picks his way through the crowded cafe 'Hey!' he says. 'You wouldn't think it could be so hard to give away free cake!'

'You should have ditched them into the nearest bin,' Lily says.

Dan frowns. 'No, I wanted to do it properly,' he says. 'Move up, Frankie, huh?' Frankie shuffles along into the seat beside Lily, and Dan flops down next to me with a wink. Lily's smile has turned upside down, but my heart just about flips over.

'I handed one to a woman whose umbrella had blown inside out,' Dan is saying. 'Then there were two little kids in wellies and a guy selling *The Big Issue* on the corner. I gave him three.'

Dan hangs the dripping angel wings on the back of his chair, grinning, and I find myself grinning right back. He shrugs off his wet jacket to reveal a tight black T-shirt with *Heaven* printed across the chest, and that's kind of appropriate as right now I think maybe I've died and gone there.

Being invisible is dangerous, obviously, because once you start to materialize again you feel pretty grateful to anyone who happens to notice you're alive. That's all it is, I tell myself. It's not like I am falling for a boy who tears up exercise books and sets fire to his desk.

Even I can see that would be a very bad idea . . .

8

I finish my last mouthful of strawberry cream sponge with a sigh.

'Oi,' Lily says, jabbing Frankie in the ribs. 'Didn't you lot say you had to be going?'

'Did we?' Frankie echoes.

'Yes, you did,' she insists. 'Places to go, things to do, that's what you said.'

'I'd better head off, anyway,' Kurt admits. 'My gran will be wondering where I am.'

'I, also,' I say. The three of us get to our feet and Lily grins and shifts along a little to sit closer to Dan. Then her face falls, because Dan stands up too, saying he can't let us go out in that rain, he'll walk with us, bring the big umbrella.

'You only just got here!' Lily protests.

'It's OK,' Dan shrugs. 'No hassle.'

Lily scowls. 'Well . . . I guess I'll come too.'

We pull on damp jackets, push our chairs under the table. 'Not leaving the wings, surely, Dan?' Frankie teases, and he laughs and pulls them on.

The cafe is quieter now, with just a few lingering customers and the little-brother waiters wiping down tabletops. A tired-looking woman with the same caramel skin as Dan is sweeping the floor.

'Won't be long,' Dan tells them. 'Five minutes, OK? I'll help you clear up.' He ruffles the hair of the littlest brother on his way out.

That's how I end up walking down Lark Lane in a downpour, squashed under a big umbrella with Frankie, Kurt, Lily and a brown-eyed boy in dripping angel wings. Lily, who has managed to hide her own umbrella, links arms with Dan.

'It must be tough, Anya,' Dan is saying. 'Starting over in a whole new country where you don't even speak the language . . .'

'Yes, it is!'

'We'll help you, though,' Frankie says. 'That's what friends are for. Right?'

Kurt and Dan nod, grinning, but Lily rolls her eyes.

'Try talking a bit more,' Kurt suggests. 'Get to know people.'

'I don't have the words,' I explain. 'Is all . . . tangled up in my head. Yes? People do not understand!'

'We understand,' Dan points out. 'Your accent's weird, but it's kind of cute too!'

I decide maybe I will try to talk more often, if Dan Carney thinks my accent is cute.

'Whatever,' Lily says crossly. 'Just don't make such a fuss about it, Anya. You'll be OK.'

For the first time since we got to England, I think maybe I will.

We leave Frankie outside her flat at the end of Lark Lane, wave goodbye to Kurt at his gran's little terraced house near the main road. Lily's house is a smart Victorian semi with a pretty front garden, the kind of place I imagined us living in, and I try not to dislike her for having what I wanted and didn't get.

She pauses beside the blue painted gate, giving Dan her sparkliest smile.

'Want to come in and dry off a bit?' she asks. 'My parents will be out till late, and I've got that new Katy Perry CD . . .'

Before Dan can answer, a light goes on inside the house and two figures can be seen moving about inside.

Lily rolls her eyes skywards. 'Oh, great,' she huffs. 'Another time, OK?'

'See you, Lily,' Dan calls, then turns to me. 'Where now?'

'Across the park,' I tell him. 'Flat above fish and chip shop.'

Now it's just Dan and me, under the umbrella, and the rest of the world seems to fade as we go through the gates into Princes Park and squelch across the grass, dodging puddles.

'Boy, am I in trouble,' Dan sighs, shaking his head. 'The school are bound to write, or ring, or something . . . I don't usually do stuff like that, Anya. I lost the plot, y'know? It's not like I was trying to burn down the school. I just didn't want to read my work out in class, that's all. No big deal.'

We walk past the boating lake, and Dan stops short, his face all frowny and anxious. 'You must think I'm a real loser.'

I shake my head. I can think of a lot of words to describe Dan Carney, but loser isn't one of them. 'No,' I tell him. 'Not a loser.'

Dan rakes a hand through ink-black hair and swears under his breath. 'How come I always get things so wrong?' he growls. 'What is it with me?'

He kicks out at a broken-down bit of wall just beside the far gate, then slumps down on to it, head in hands. I stand for a moment in the pouring rain, then Dan tilts the umbrella and pats the wall beside him and I sit down too. The wall is damp and cold and uneven, but it doesn't seem to matter because Dan is right next to me. The umbrella tilts forward, shielding us from the world, so that just our legs and boots stick out into the rain.

'I feel like a loser,' Dan huffs. 'It's just . . . Miss Matthews asked us to write about personal stuff, right? Then she asked us to read it out, but private stuff is supposed to stay private! I didn't want the whole class knowing my business. So when Lily handed me the lighter . . . I didn't even think, I just wanted to get rid of what I'd written. When I get angry, I act first and think later. Big mistake, huh?'

That's kind of an understatement. Dan must have wanted to keep his writing secret pretty badly if he was ready to set fire to it rather than read it out in class.

'Bet Fisher excludes me,' Dan says, kicking out a bit of crumbling brickwork. 'Mum'll be really upset, and Dad will go crazy, and things will get even worse at home. Nightmare. Stupid cafe. Stupid Dad. Stupid school . . .'

The dark, scowly frown fades from Dan's face and he sighs heavily, shoulders slumped. Now he doesn't look angry so much as lost, a sad-eyed boy in wet angel wings with all the cares of the world on his shoulders. He looks at me sideways.

'Don't know why I'm telling you all this,' he says. 'You don't even know what I'm saying, do you? Not all of it, anyway. Just as well. I'm not much of an angel, that's for sure.'

I want to tell Dan that I understand a lot more than he thinks, but I can't find the words, so I just smile. Dan smiles back, his brown eyes shining, and then, before I can even see it coming, he leans across and kisses me softly.

I have never been kissed before.

Dan Carney smells of milkshake and vanilla. The umbrella drops to the ground and cold rain falls on us like confetti, but Dan's lips are warm and sweet as sugar frosting. Then he pulls back, moving away from me.

'Hey,' he says. 'We'd better get you home.'

Home? My mind has emptied of everything except Dan. I don't want to come back into the real world, but Dan seems to be in a hurry. He scoops up the umbrella and pulls me to my feet. 'Where did you say you lived?' he asks. 'The flat over the chippy, right?'

He takes my hand, steering me through the park gates and across the road. The chip-shop windows are streaming with rain, and the hot stink of frying fish drifts out as we stand on the pavement, discarded chip wrappers at our feet.

Dan frowns. 'One thing you should know about me, Anya – I'm kind of a mess, OK? Bad news.'

'Bad news?' I echo.

'Sorry, Anya . . . I'll see you around.'

He walks away, crossing the wasteground that's littered with broken glass and scrunched-up chip papers, hunched under the big white umbrella.

9

That's the day I begin to believe in miracles. Nothing has changed, but everything has . . . all because of a boy in angel wings.

My life is still a disaster zone. I am still sharing a room with my little sister in a scabby flat where the smell of chip fat and vinegar clings to everything, but none of that seems to matter any more . . . because of Dan.

I lie awake late into the night, listening to the sound of people outside, laughing, singing, fighting. When I sleep, my dreams are full of a tall boy with caramel skin and angel wings, a boy who kissed me in the rain.

The next day I go to school with a little less dread in my heart. My heart races a little as I walk through the corridors, but there's no sign of Dan. He's not in the corridors, he's not in class, he's not in the canteen . . . Dan Carney has vanished.

Frankie flops down next to me at lunchtime. It looks like I have a new friend – we bonded over the strawberry meringues, a match made in Heaven. Frankie is an outsider, a misfit, a million miles away from Nadia and the cool, popular kids I knew back in Krakow . . . but then I'm kind of a misfit myself, these days. The laughing, pink-cheeked, hockey-mad girls I imagined I'd meet don't seem to exist outside the pages of the books Dad used to send me.

'So . . . Dan Carney is gone?' I ask her, trying to be casual. 'In trouble?'

'Big trouble,' she says, biting into a hot dog. 'He's been excluded. Mr Fisher takes that whole burn-the-school-down stuff very seriously.'

'Excluded?'

'Banned from school for a few days,' Frankie explains. 'Still, it'll take more than that to change Dan.'

The disappointment must show in my face, because Frankie starts to grin. 'Wait a minute, Anya . . . he was flirting with you, right? In the cafe? Don't tell me you've fallen for him!'

'Dan is a friendly boy,' I whisper.

Frankie snorts. 'How friendly, exactly?'

I can't quite meet her eye. 'In the park, we talk. And then –'

'He didn't kiss you – did he?' she squeals.

I bite my lip.

Frankie shakes her head. 'Seriously, Anya, don't

go there. Dan is bad news . . . a scally, a troublemaker. He's not boyfriend material. Don't be fooled by the angel wings.'

'I won't,' I promise, even though I know it's already too late.

On Wednesday, a letter arrives from Krakow. I recognize Nadia's curly handwriting and rip it open, grinning, but the smile soon fades. Nadia's upbeat chat makes me feel a million miles away from my old friends, and I guess that's exactly what I am.

When I read the bit about Agatta moving into my old scat next to Nadia, my eyes blur with tears. Well, what did I expect? That Nadia would go on sitting next to an empty desk, just because I happened to move away?

What would Nadia say about Dan Carney? What would she say about Frankie, and Kurt? I'm not sure she'd be impressed with any of them, but that's too bad.

They're all I have right now.

That afternoon, I drag Kazia along to the park, hoping to bump into Dan, but it's empty except for a few shivering mums with kids in pushchairs. The next day it's the same. The day after that, pining for a glimpse of melted chocolate eyes, braided hair and slanting caramel cheekbones, I find one of the free cake vouchers in my blazer pocket and take Kazia along to the cafe.

I have a lot of questions, questions I just couldn't ask Frankie. If a boy kisses you, doesn't that mean something? Like, maybe you're going out? In Krakow, it would mean that, but Liverpool might be different. Still, shouldn't Dan have been in touch by now? He didn't ask for my phone number, but maybe he could call at the flat or something . . . anything?

We push open the cafe door, find ourselves a corner seat. Dan's mum is there, and the little brothers, but there is no sign of Dan. Kazia and I share a milkshake and eat frosted cupcakes, and finally I pluck up the courage to ask one of the brothers where Dan is.

'He's not well,' the boy tells me solemnly. 'He's got the flu.'

I blink. Excluded from school *and* ill? Maybe that's why I haven't heard from him.

I tell Frankie this next day, at breaktime.

'I bet the flu is just a cover-up!' she says. 'Dan's parents probably don't even know he's been excluded! That boy is such a chancer!'

She narrows her eyes. 'How come you were at the cafe, anyhow?' she wants to know. 'You weren't looking for him, were you? Anya, that's not how it works! Besides, you promised you wouldn't fall for him!'

'Fall for who?' Kurt asks, wandering up to join us.

'Nobody,' I say.

'Dan,' Frankie says, and Kurt raises an eyebrow.

I wish the floor would open up and swallow me.

'He's trouble,' Frankie insists. 'He was OK the other day, with the cakes and the umbrella and stuff . . . that was a surprise, I admit. Mostly, though, he's mad, bad and dangerous to know . . . that's boys for you, I guess.'

'What d'you mean?' Kurt protests.

Frankie sighs. 'Never trust a boy, that's what my mum says,' she tells us. 'They lie, cheat, break your heart and then disappear and leave you to clean up the mess.'

'Dan's not like that,' I say.

'They're *all* like that,' Frankie insists.

'How come your mum thinks boys are such bad news?' Kurt wants to know.

Frankie shrugs. 'Dad left us when I was a kid,' she explains. 'We never saw him again. Mum had to do the whole parenthood thing alone.'

'I'm not like that,' Kurt says.

'Well, no, that's for sure,' Frankie says. 'You're just a weirdo geek with a mania for small furry animals.'

'You love me really,' he grins.

'Can't help myself,' Frankie laughs. 'Anyway . . . speaking of small furry animals, how is Cheesy? Settling in?'

59

'He's fine.'

Frankie glances over at Lily Caldwell, lounging against a radiator, checking her sparkly eyeshadow – blue today – in a little mirror. 'Lily's kept quiet about it too,' she whispers. 'That's a miracle. I was expecting blackmail notes at the very least.'

'Lily's not so bad,' Kurt says.

'Not so bad?' Frankie snorts. 'Have you forgotten what she says about you . . . and me?'

'Not recently,' Kurt says.

'Well, no, not in the last few days . . .'

Lily has stayed away from Frankie, Kurt and me since that wet afternoon at Heaven, and that's a good thing. No more quips about Frankie's weight or Kurt's clothes. No more comments about sauerkraut. We have become a no-go area for Lily's barbed tongue, but it's clear she finds the three of us about as interesting as algebra or drying paint.

'Anyway,' Kurt says. 'I've nearly finished the secret rat cage . . .' Kurt's gran is terrified of rats, so he needs to keep Cheesy hidden. With this in mind, he is converting his wardrobe into a gigantic rat's cage. 'I just need some chicken wire and it'll be sorted.'

'Kurt,' Frankie says gently. 'What if your gran opens the wardrobe door one day to hang up a pair of those scary trousers of yours . . . and sees Cheesy? Won't she be a bit . . . shocked?'

'She won't find him,' Kurt insists. 'I told her I'd

be looking after my own clothes from now on. Doing my own washing and ironing and putting away. It's foolproof.'

Frankie and I exchange looks, then dissolve into giggles. 'I hope so,' I say. 'Rat in wardrobe . . . this is not good!'

A week ago, I was pining for Krakow. I'd given up on Liverpool, but maybe I was wrong?

After all, back then I'd never hidden a rat in my satchel or had an after-school detention or eaten cake with pink sugar frosting. A week ago, I didn't dare to hope I might be chatting and giggling with my friends, even if they are kind of geeky and odd, the kind of kids I'd never have given a second glance to back home.

Well, things move on – Nadia's letter showed me that much.

It's good to laugh, and it's good to have friends. It's a start, anyhow.

10

Dan Carney is back. It's Monday morning and he's swaggering down the school corridor, surrounded by laughing boys in baggy trousers and studded belts, boys with swirling tramlines shaved into their ultra-short hair, boys with expensive trainers and designer-label hoodies. They punch Dan lightly, ruffle his braided hair, tell him he's the coolest. Nobody, they remind him, ever tried to burn down the school before.

Dan just laughs.

And right in the middle of the bad-boy gang, her arm linked through Dan's, is Lily Caldwell. She is wearing strappy ankle boots with skyscraper heels and a skirt so short it's more of a very wide belt. Her lashes are so thick with mascara it looks like she has whole families of tarantulas stuck to her eyelids.

My heart thumps and my cheeks glow pink. I have waited almost a week to see Dan again, and now he's back, arm in arm with the meanest girl in the year, and I haven't a clue what to say.

'Hello' doesn't really seem to cover it.

I just stand still, hugging my satchel, as the bad-boy gang sweeps past. Right at the last moment Dan catches my eye and my heart leaps, but his brown eyes look right through me as if I don't exist.

I wasn't sure what Frankie meant when she told me Dan was bad news, but I know now, and it hurts. It hurts so much that my eyes blur with tears, and I almost miss the smug grin Lily throws me over her shoulder as the whole bunch of them turn the corner and disappear.

Frankie takes my elbow. 'Hey, hey,' she says softly. 'What did I tell you? Never trust a boy.'

She hands me a tissue and I wipe my eyes, dredge up a smile. 'Better?' she checks. 'Don't take it personally, Anya. Kids like Dan and Lily don't bother with the likes of us, not usually. Maybe outside of school they'll be OK, once in a while, but inside these walls they have an image to keep up. You'll never see Lily Caldwell being nice to the likes of you and me, or Dan Carney bothering to notice we're alive. It's just the way things are.'

'But . . . why?'

Frankie rolls her eyes. 'There's this whole king-of-the-jungle thing going on at school,' she explains. 'At this school, anyway. The lions are in charge – they're at the top of the heap. They just have to roar and everyone jumps to attention. That's what

Lily and Dan are, see? Then you get elephants and antelope and herds of wildebeest and stuff, who are all a bit scared of the lions . . .'

Jungle, zoo . . . I was right about the wild animals bit, anyhow.

'What are we?' I ask, my voice still shaky. 'What are you, me and Kurt, in this jungle?'

'We're zebra and lemurs and parrots,' Frankie says. 'The cool, interesting ones.'

'Yes?'

'Yeah, but Lily and Dan don't realize that,' she frowns. 'To them, we're right at the bottom of the pile. Ants and frogs and minnows. And we don't mix. Mess with the lions and they'll eat you up!'

'I know Lily does not like me,' I say. 'But I thought Dan was different!'

'No,' Frankie says. 'He's not. Don't kid yourself.'

I guess that's exactly what I've been doing. I let myself believe in miracles, even though I know they don't exist. What was I, to Dan? A girl who didn't understand the language, the rules, the law of the jungle. A girl who didn't matter, invisible, forgettable.

'What shall I do, Frankie?' I ask.

Frankie sighs. 'Blank him,' she says. 'Ignore him. OK?'

All through maths and French, I doodle in the margins of my exercise books, torturing myself with questions. I've heard of girls being dumped after just one date, but just one kiss? It may be a new world record.

What was so awful about me, anyway? Was I too sad, too silent, too serious for a boy like Dan? Did my breath taste sour or stale? I'm certain it didn't. Maybe my kissing technique was bad?

At least Dan isn't in maths or French to witness my gloom. PSE is a different story.

'Ignore him,' Frankie tells me as we file into class. 'He's not worth it.'

'Not worth what?' Kurt pipes up, but Frankie tells him he wouldn't understand. We sit down near the front, and Dan, Lily and a few of the scally-boy crew mooch in late. Dan's eyes catch mine again, and this time I could swear they flicker with something dark, unspoken, before sliding away.

Dan and his friends slouch into seats at the back while Miss Matthews clears her throat and tries not to look anxious. The whole lesson is one big joke to the bad-boy gang. 'Hey, Dan,' one of them smirks. 'You're all *fired up* today, aren't you?'

'Maybe, maybe not,' Dan grins. 'That's the *burning question*!'

There's the sound of tearing paper from the back row, and Lily sniggers and asks if anyone has a lighter. Miss Matthews doesn't relax until the bell goes to signal the end of the lesson – well, maybe she's just relieved it's not the fire alarm. At least nothing has been burned, charred, torched or fried – except perhaps her nerves.

Dan slouches up to the desk and drops a crumpled paper on to it. 'I'm on report, Miss,' he says. 'You have to sign to say I behaved in class.'

Miss Matthews sighs. 'And did you behave?' she asks.

'Erm . . .'

'Let's just say you were no angel,' Frankie mutters, packing her bag. 'Better hang up your wings, hoodie-boy.'

Dan dredges up what might be a guilty look.

'I'll try harder next time,' he tells the teacher. 'Can you sign it? Please?'

Miss Matthews signs the sheet, and Dan slopes off. Frankie, Kurt and I head for the door, but Miss Matthews calls me back.

'Anya?' she says. 'Can I have a word?'

I pause by her desk. Miss Matthews takes my exercise book from the pile and opens it. Suddenly I remember writing about my first day here, about kids like wild animals who yell and roar and stampede through the corridors, ranting, frantic teachers, lessons that made no sense at all. Oops.

'I am in trouble?' I ask.

'Trouble?' she repeats. 'No, no, of course not!'

'My English is not good,' I whisper. 'I get things wrong . . .'

'Anya, this is a wonderful piece of writing. The spelling and grammar aren't perfect, but your feelings jump off the page. It shows a far greater grasp of English than I expected. You have a talent!'

I blink. 'I do?'

'You do. And now that we know what you can do, perhaps you will try to take part a little more in other classes? Show all your teachers what you can do?'

'I will try . . .'

'I can see now how hard these past few weeks have been for you,' Miss Matthews says. 'I didn't quite realize – I don't think anybody did. But you will settle, Anya. And I'm here for you, if you need to talk, if you ever have any problems. Do you understand?'

I nod, blinking back my shock as I pick up my satchel. 'Thank you, Miss Matthews,' I say. 'Thank you!'

I walk out into the corridor, my head high, my heart a little lighter than before. Dan Carney is lurking just outside the classroom, minus his friends. He rakes a hand through unruly black braids, takes a step towards me, but it's my turn now to look right through him, just like Frankie said.

I walk on down the corridor, to where Frankie and Kurt are waiting.

When I get home from school, Dan Carney is leaning against the lamp post just across from the flat, eating chips.

'Hey, Anya,' he grins.

I remember this morning, the way Dan's laughing eyes looked straight through me and turned my heart to ice, and I walk past him as if I didn't hear. With shaking fingers, I fit my key into the lock and step inside. I run up the stairs, creep into my bedroom and peer out from behind the threadbare curtains.

He's still there.

I let the curtain drop. Today Dan Carney ignored me at school, but now he's eating chips just across the road from where I live, grinning.

There are some things I just don't understand about Britain, and the weirdo language is only one of them. Words, they're not so complicated . . . but there's a whole raft of other stuff going on that is a mystery to me.

Like how come Kurt is so smart and funny, yet

68

can't sort himself out a decent pair of trousers. How come Frankie moans that she's fat and then scoffs chips each lunchtime, with crisps and pudding and Coke as well. And how come Dan Carney kissed me in the rain, as if he really meant it, then changed his mind and cut me dead at school today, left me stranded in the corridor with an ache where my heart should be.

Maybe I'm trying so hard to work out what people are saying that I am missing the little things, the clues other people pick up on to read between the lines? I met a boy in angel wings and forgot that he was the kind of boy who tears up school books and sets things on fire, the kind of boy you don't mess with unless you want to get your fingers burnt.

And now he's turned into a stalker too.

Mum and Kazia come in. 'There's a boy sitting on the steps,' Kazia tells me. 'He's says he's a friend of yours.'

'He isn't,' I say.

Mum raises an eyebrow. She looks tired. Cleaning hotel rooms is not the nicest way to make a living, but she never complains. She makes soup for supper, mixes up some sourdough to make rye bread that will be fresh and warm when Dad gets home. By the time he arrives, the bread is cooling on the rack, and it's been dark for an hour.

'Anya,' he says, 'there's a boy outside who says he's waiting for you. What's going on?'

'He's just a boy from school,' I say. 'Nobody.'

We eat bowls of rich beetroot soup and hunks of warm, tangy bread that tastes like home, and Kazia peers out of the window again.

'He's still there,' she reports. 'Is he your boyfriend?'

'No, he is not! I wish he'd go away!'

'Do you want me to go out and tell him?' Dad asks.

I shake my head, defeated. 'I'll do it.'

I drag a comb through my hair, pull on boots and a thick jumper. I run downstairs and open the door.

Dan Carney is sitting on the step.

'Finally,' he says, getting to his feet. 'I thought you'd never come down. I've eaten two bags of chips, a portion of curry sauce and four onion rings, but it's freezing cold and I'm down to my last few pennies. And I think I've got indigestion.'

Those soft brown eyes could melt an iceberg. 'Why are you here?' I ask.

'We're friends, aren't we?' Dan says brightly. 'And you're new to Liverpool . . . I thought I might give you a guided tour.'

'No, thank you,' I say.

Dan looks hurt. 'Why not?' he asks.

'I cannot trust you,' I tell him. 'One minute, you

try to burn up the school. Then angel wings and cake. Then . . . nothing!'

'I'm complicated,' Dan says. 'Is that a problem?'

Well, just a bit. I turn to go back inside, but Dan catches my arm.

'Don't go,' he says. 'Look, I'm sorry, OK? Sorry I haven't been in touch. Sorry about today. Don't be mad at me!'

I look up into his melted chocolate eyes, and somehow I forget to be angry.

'Can we talk? Please, Anya?' he says.

The two of us sit on the doorstep. Little kids are riding their bikes up and down the street, steering with one hand or no hands at all, swooping out into the lamplight, then skidding back into the darkness.

'I'm all the things you said,' Dan admits. 'I just – well, I don't much like school. And I get angry, sometimes.'

'Why?' I ask.

Dan shrugs. 'Just . . . stuff. I'll tell you, some day. I'm not all bad, honest.'

'I know that.'

'You can trust me,' he says.

'Maybe.'

'So, am I forgiven?' Dan smiles, and every last bit of resistance melts away. I grin at him.

'C'mon,' he says, dragging me to my feet. A curtain twitches in my bedroom, and I catch a glimpse of Kazia, peeking out. 'A guided tour of Liverpool,' Dan is saying. 'Let's go!'

'No, Dan,' I laugh. 'Not tonight. It is late, and dark. I have homework –'

'Homework?' Dan frowns, as if he's never heard of such a thing.

'I have lots of work to do,' I tell him. 'I must practise my English, catch up with lessons . . .'

'Seriously?' Dan asks. 'You're not coming out?'

I shake my head.

'Tomorrow then?' he tries instead. 'We'll start tomorrow! I want to show you that Liverpool can be fun!'

'Dan, I . . .'

I want to tell him that this is a bad idea. We are too different to be friends, the bad boy and the quiet girl who can't even string a few sentences together. And I don't want to risk being hurt again, which means that going anywhere with Dan Carney would be a bad, bad idea. My head aches, trying to put together the verbs and adjectives, and when my mouth opens, everything goes wrong.

'OK,' I tell him. 'This sounds . . . good!'

'Cool!' His soft brown eyes twinkle. 'See you then,' he says.

Never trust a boy, isn't that what Frankie said? I guess I should have listened.

Dan Carney is not in school the next day, and although I'm half expecting to find him camped out on my doorstep after 3.30, there's no sign of him.

I start some maths homework, then some art. Still no Dan.

'Why d'you keep looking out of the window?' Kazia wants to know. 'Are you looking for that weird boy?'

'No,' I snap. 'I'm not looking for anyone!'

I don't have any more homework, but I remember Miss Matthews's advice. I open my exercise book and write a couple of pages about Krakow. Still no Dan.

Dad is even later home tonight, so we don't eat supper till eight. Kazia and I wash up, then I iron some clothes for school and go to bed, wishing I had never heard of Dan Carney.

12

There's a faint ringing noise, like the sound of a demented mobile, tugging me from sleep. Then silence. I sigh and stretch and drag the blankets over my head, and then it's back, a shrill, chirpy sound, nagging, persistent.

I sit up. The room is still, except for Kazia's muffled breathing in the bed across from me. The noise must be coming from outside. It's too thin and reedy to be a car alarm. It sounds like . . . a bicycle bell.

I slide out of bed and run over to the window, lifting up the corner of the threadbare curtain. There on the pavement, in a pool of yellow light from the street lamp, is Dan Carney, wearing angel wings, astride a big old-fashioned bike with a basket fixed to the front of it. He rings the bell again, grinning up at me.

I pull on my pink fluffy slippers and grab a coat, creep past Mum and Dad's bedroom and down the creaky stairs. I open the door and slip outside, shivering in the cold night air.

'What are you doing?' I whisper. 'It's the middle of the night!'

'You said you liked the angel wings,' Dan shrugs. 'So here I am. Just didn't want people to think I make a habit of all this feathery stuff, OK? I have a reputation to keep up. So . . . well, I figured there wouldn't be many people around to see me at this time of night.'

He notices my fluffy slippers and spotty pyjamas, frowning. 'Um . . . are you ready?'

'Ready?' I echo.

Dan looks confused. 'The guided tour,' he says. 'It was all arranged. You agreed!'

'But it is so late!' I protest. 'Everyone is asleep!'

Dan laughs. 'Exactly,' he tells me. 'We have the whole city to ourselves, practically. C'mon!'

'I cannot!' I argue. 'My family!'

'They're asleep, you said so yourself,' Dan says. 'Besides, you promised. And I borrowed the bike specially. C'mon!'

Before I know what's happening, Dan slides his arms round me and hauls me up on to the crossbar of the bike. 'No!' I yelp. 'Dan! I cannot!'

But Dan isn't listening. He launches the bike off the pavement and out along the road, wobbling slightly. I shift position, grab on to the handlebars with one hand and Dan with the other. I have never ridden on the crossbar of a rickety old bike before, or been kidnapped either, for that matter. I guess there is a first time for everything.

I'm surprised to find I'm smiling.

'So,' Dan says, steering the bike round on to the wide, tree-lined avenue that leads into town, pedalling faster. 'This is Princes Boulevard. It's where all the rich people used to live, like a hundred years ago. Mostly flats now, though. Can you imagine it with horses and carriages and crinoline dresses? Liverpool was dead posh, once.'

The breeze ruffles my hair and lifts it out behind me. I gaze up at the crumbling terraced houses with their big bay windows and litter-strewn gardens and try to imagine them a hundred years ago. What would those long-gone people make of us, a boy in angel wings and a girl in pyjamas, riding through the night on an antique bicycle? We pedal on.

'Hang on,' Dan says. 'We're turning . . .'

The bike wobbles slightly as we take the corner, and I fall back against Dan before getting my balance again. A huge, dark building towers over us suddenly, vast and terrifying. Spotlights cast an orange glow over its ancient gothic arches and pinnacles.

It's a little like the elegant, ancient churches we

have back in Krakow, but squarer, more solid, somehow.

'This is the Anglican cathedral,' Dan says. 'Spooky, huh? They do good tea and scones in the cafe . . . not at night, obviously. And not as good as the ones Mum makes!'

We ride on through the dark, deserted streets. Dan points out the Catholic cathedral, which I know already from Sunday Mass, the university, art college, even the Jewish synagogue. Then we cycle back along Princes Boulevard and swoop down into the park. Dan takes a blanket from the bike basket, spreading it out over the dew-wet grass beside the boating lake, and unfolds a parcel of iced cakes wrapped in a red-checked tea towel.

'Breakfast,' he tells me. 'Like it?'

'It's perfect, Dan. Thank you!'

'This is just the start . . . a taster, if you like,' Dan says. He picks up one of the little cupcakes and bites into it, grinning. 'There's loads more I can show you. Liverpool's cool. Seriously!'

As I bite into the golden sponge cake and the sweet, melty frosting, I can almost believe him. The sky above us pales, and watercolour washes of pink and gold and orange seep over the horizon. Trees that looked skinny and stunted in daylight seem tall and elegant now, their branches silhouetted against the dawn.

I guess even the most unlikely places can feel

special, if you're with the right person – or if you know how to look.

Right now, though, I'm tired . . . and worried too. If Mum and Dad discover I'm missing, they'll go crazy.

'I must go,' I whisper, and Dan just smiles and gets to his feet, shaking out the blanket, lifting the bike upright again.

As we ride out through the park gates, a little milk float is buzzing its way along the street. Cartons of milk have already been left on the step by the door of the flat.

'Hang on to me, really tight,' Dan says, and I lean into him, waiting for a jolt or a wobble or a swerve. It doesn't happen. The bike comes to a slow, smooth halt outside the flat.

'Why must I hold tight?' I ask, and Dan just laughs.

'Because I like it when you do,' he says. 'I guess you can let go now, Anya. If you really want to . . .'

'Dan!' I protest. I slide to the pavement, and he adjusts the white-feathered wings and rides away, grinning. I bend and pick up the milk. The door to the flat swings open and Dad appears, dressed for work.

'Anya,' he says, surprised. 'You're up early . . . I didn't hear you moving about. Were you collecting the milk?'

'Mmm,' I say, hiding the lie with a yawn.

'Good girl. I thought I'd get an early start today. There are a few things I need to sort out. I'll try not to be so late back tonight.'

Dad kisses the top of my head and walks away, and I slip into the flat just as the clock turns seven.

13

There is just one problem with going out to watch the dawn . . . it kind of wrecks you for school the next day.

I yawn all the way through French and maths and finally fall asleep in history. Frankie jabs me in the ribs just as I am dreaming of picnics in the park in my pyjamas with a boy who may or may not be an angel.

'Wake up,' she hisses. 'At least pretend to listen. What's up with you?'

'Sorry,' I whisper. 'I had a late night. Dan came over . . .'

Frankie's eyes are wide. 'Whoa . . . be careful, Anya. I've told you before . . . that boy is bad news.'

'Frances McGee!' Mr Goldman yells, and she snaps to attention, blinking. 'I'm sure you've been listening carefully. Perhaps you'd like to tell the class the causes of the Great Fire of London?'

Frankie doesn't miss a beat. 'Wasn't that Dan Carney, Sir?'

The class dissolves into giggles. 'Most amusing,' Mr Goldman huffs. 'Where is Dan, anyway? Our little arsonist not here today?'

A few of the bad-boy crew at the back of the class offer random excuses for Dan. He's broken his leg, he's at the dentist, he's been expelled forever for setting fire to Mr Fisher's Burberry raincoat. Mr Goldman rolls his eyes.

I have a strong feeling Dan is still curled up in bed, asleep, his wings hanging from the coat stand.

'Watch out, Anya,' Frankie says later in the school canteen, flicking through a music magazine, one where all the bands seem to be young and skinny and dressed in black. 'I like Dan, but he should have a government health warning stamped all over him. Don't get involved.'

'Involved in what?' Kurt wants to know.

'Girl stuff,' Frankie scoffs. 'Crushes, kisses . . . true lurve. You wouldn't understand.'

'How do you know?' Kurt protests.

'I just do,' Frankie says. 'Seriously, Anya, Dan's no angel.'

But he's the only good thing in my life right now, the only thing that makes this place bearable. And sometimes I see a sweet, sad, gentle side to Dan, a side I know Frankie has never seen. Sometimes he makes me miserable, sometimes he makes me mad, but he can make my heart flip over with just one look. And last night was special . . . so special.

'You're not even listening, are you?' Frankie sighs.

'It's OK, Anya. Love is deaf, as well as blind,' Kurt says wisely. 'Anyone want a banana chip?' He offers us a bag of dried brownish discs, and I take one, just to be polite. It tastes like something that may have been a banana, once, very long ago. Possibly in a past life.

Kurt is always trying to tempt us into healthy eating with beansprout sandwiches, tofu quiche and random shrivelled things masquerading as fruit. It's not really working, so far.

'Yuck,' Frankie sniffs. 'Why call it a banana chip when it tastes nothing like either? It's more like old shoe leather. If this is healthy eating, I'd rather be fat.'

'You're not fat!' Kurt says. 'You're just cuddly. In a nice way.'

Frankie's lip curls.

'Get a grip,' she snaps. 'I am not cuddly, I'm fat. Don't go getting any ideas, OK? You are so not my type, Kurt Jones. It's not just the drooping handknitted school jumpers and the hideous trousers, either. You do equations for fun, and eat vile, shrivelled things that even Cheesy wouldn't bother with –'

'What do you mean . . . hideous trousers?' Kurt asks, in injured tones.

'You must know,' she sighs. 'You get teased about them often enough.'

'I don't mind being a bit different . . .'

Frankie rolls her eyes. 'There's different,' she explains, 'and there's just plain embarrassing. Ever thought of going goth?'

'Er, no . . .'

'Emo? Scene? Nu-rave?' Frankie continues. 'Punk, maybe?'

I don't even know what those things are, and I don't think Kurt does, either. 'I'm not really a punk kind of a person,' he protests.

Frankie chucks her magazine down. 'Face it, Kurt,' she says. 'You need a wardrobe makeover – and I'm not talking about rats or chicken wire.'

She goes up to the counter for a second helping of sponge pudding and custard, and Kurt picks up the magazine, sulking. 'Look at these people,' he says, baffled. 'All that backcombed hair, those skinny trousers. Does Frankie really like all that?'

I bite my lip. 'I think she does,' I tell him.

'She'd like me better if I looked like . . . like this?' Kurt says, peering at a poster of a wild-eyed singer with eyeliner and heavily tattooed arms. 'I will never understand girls.'

'Frankie is strange,' I shrug. 'But she does like you, Kurt.'

'I don't know about that,' Kurt says gloomily.

'She never even noticed I was alive until recently.'

I've been invisible myself, and silent too, so I know how Kurt is feeling.

'We don't have anything in common,' Kurt sighs, toying with a slice of lentil quiche. 'We're too different.'

'Different is good,' I say, thinking of me and Dan.

'I'm not just different, I'm dull,' Kurt says. 'That's what Frankie thinks.'

'Not dull,' I tell him. 'But if Frankie thinks so, then why not surprise her? You are a smart boy. Think about it. What does Frankie like? What will please her?'

Frankie is coming back to the table with a double helping of sponge pudding and custard, a contented smile on her face.

Kurt begins to grin. 'Hey, Frankie,' he says. 'I was just saying to Anya, I wonder how that crazy cafe is getting on? D'you fancy going along after school, to check it out? I'll buy you both a cake!'

Frankie raises an eyebrow. 'I thought lentils and miso soup were more your thing?' she asks.

'They are,' Kurt agrees. 'But those cakes at Heaven are something else . . .'

'Go on then,' Frankie grins. 'We'll come, right, Anya?'

I smile, but my heart starts up a drumbeat that has nothing to do with Kurt or Frankie. Maybe Dan will be there . . . and maybe, after last night, even Frankie will see that he's the boy for me.

Maybe.

14

Heaven

A big yellow cab with a slanting tower welded on to its roof is parked right outside Heaven. It looks like a taxi that's been badly customized with gloss paint and some random freestyle roof-sculpture. *Yellow Submarine Beatles Tours* is painted in rainbow shades along the sides.

'Scary,' Frankie says. 'This place gets weirder by the minute.'

Inside, the cafe is almost deserted. Angel-boy Dan is wiping down the tabletops while his little brothers are doing homework at a table in the corner. He looks up with a grin that makes my toes melt.

'Hey, Anya,' he says. 'Hi, Frankie, Kurt.'

'No wings today?' Frankie quips. 'Is that because you've been skiving school again?'

'Shhh!' Dan says in a loud whisper, looking round to check his little brothers aren't listening. 'I wasn't skiving, I was helping out. I told Mum there was a class trip to Alton Towers, and she let me stay off . . .'

'Bad boy, Dan,' Frankie says, shaking her head. 'No wonder your halo's slipped . . .'

We order Coke floats and cupcakes and settle ourselves at the window table. The only other customer is an ageing hippy in an orange satin coat, sitting in the far corner eating a cheese sandwich from a plastic lunchbox.

'Hey!' Frankie whispers as Dan arrives back with the drinks and cakes. 'He's eating his own butties!'

'Oh, that's Ringo,' Dan explains. 'He's a Beatles tour guide, and he's started taking his breaks in here –'

Frankie snorts. 'Don't tell me, that hideous taxi-thing belongs to him, right?'

'It's a yellow submarine, like in the Beatles song,' Dan says. 'He brought in a bunch of American tourists yesterday, and they had nine cakes and four giant lattes between them, so we pretend not to notice when he gets the cheese butties out.'

'You're nuts,' Frankie mutters. 'It's a wonder you make any money at all . . .'

A bell chimes as the cafe door swings open and a posse of teenagers come in – Lily Caldwell and some of Dan's scally friends from school. She looks across and takes in the scene, then leans over and stubs out her ciggy on my cake plate. 'Sorry,' she says, not sounding it at all.

'You're not supposed to smoke in here,' one of

Dan's little brothers pipes up, but Lily just gives him a cold stare and he shrugs and goes back to his homework.

'Comin' out, mate?' one of the lads asks. His eyes scan the half-empty cafe, lingering with distaste on Ringo. 'C'mon, Dan, this place is dead!'

'I'm working,' Dan says. 'Y'know how it is.'

'You could skive off,' another says. 'We're goin' into town!'

'Sorry, not tonight,' Dan shrugs. 'Like I said.'

Lily flicks back her tawny curls. 'Just thought we'd drop in,' she says softly. 'We missed you at school today. Sure you won't come out with us? It'd be fun, promise!'

'I'm sure it would, Lily,' Dan says. 'But . . . no.'

Lily's face hardens. Her eyes catch mine, cold and mean, and I realize something. I don't much like Lily Caldwell, but she really, *really* doesn't like me.

'Suit yourself,' she says, and the whole gang of them are gone, the door slamming shut behind them. Dan grabs the plate with the stubbed-out ciggy on it, brushing the whole lot into the bin just as his mum comes out from the kitchen, wiping floury hands on her apron.

'What was that?' she asks. 'I thought we had people in!'

'Just the wind slamming the door,' Dan says. 'Sorry.'

The little brothers look up, exchanging glances, but Dan draws a finger across his throat when his mum isn't looking, and the brothers keep their mouths closed.

'I've seen you before, haven't I?' Dan's mum says, smiling at us. 'On our first day. I'm Karen Carney – it's good to meet Dan's friends from school.'

Dan's real 'friends from school' are slouching off down the street as we speak, Lily lighting up a new cigarette and the boys playing a noisy game of football with an old tin can. I drag my eyes back to Dan's mum.

'So, how was the school trip?' she asks.

'Trip?'

'You remember,' Dan prompts. 'Alton Towers.'

'Ah,' Frankie grins. 'Unforgettable, I'd say. Shame Dan couldn't make it!'

'It's nice to see that Dan has such good friends,' Karen Carney smiles. 'There are some real scallies at that school. Ringo was telling me that someone tried to set fire to the place the other week! Probably while you were off with the flu, Dan. Can you believe it?'

'I did hear something,' Kurt says. 'Terrible!'

'Who would *do* a thing like that?' Frankie wonders out loud.

Dan, who has turned a kind of dark crimson colour, looks like he wants to slip through a crack in the lino.

'There are some bad boys at school,' I blurt, trying to rescue him. 'But Dan is a good boy. Like . . . angel.'

Frankie chokes on her cream meringue, but Karen Carney doesn't seem to notice. She grins at me and her tired brown eyes are warm and sparkly. 'Well . . . I'm very lucky with my boys, I know,' she says. 'It was lovely to meet you all again! Call in any time!'

She heads back to the kitchen while Dan sinks down on to the window sill, hiding his face in his hands.

'The flu?' Frankie sniggers. 'And Alton Towers, and scallies who set fire to the school . . . very interesting!'

'She doesn't know you were excluded, does she?' Kurt says.

'How about I say the cakes are on me, if you forget everything you just heard?' Dan pleads. 'Free cakes for life? As a symbol of our lasting friendship?'

'It's a deal,' Frankie grins.

I put down my cupcake, half-eaten. Frankie and Kurt are laughing with Dan, but as I watch him bribe his way out of the tangle of lies, there's a bad taste in my mouth that even the sweet sugar frosting can't hide.

Dan told me himself, he's complicated. Right

now he's cute and kind, but at school he's a bad boy . . . about as bad as it's possible to be.

Which version is the real Dan?

I haven't a clue . . .

15

Two days later, Kurt comes into school wearing skinny black cords and a silver studded belt, and Frankie just about faints with shock.

'Anya!' she hisses, grabbing on to my arm. 'Look at that!'

'New trousers!' I breathe. 'It's a miracle!'

'He looks so . . . different!' Frankie says. 'I mean . . . not so geeky. Not so lame.'

Some of the Year Seven girls must think so too, because they give Kurt a double take as he swaggers past, then fall into a huddle, giggling and pink-cheeked.

'So,' says Kurt, ditching his rucksack at our feet and giving us a little twirl. 'New kecks. What d'you think?'

'Just call me a genius,' Frankie says. 'Seriously, I should be a stylist or something. Good to see you're taking my advice at last!'

'It's cool,' I tell Kurt. 'Already you have some admirers, I think!'

Kurt looks back at the group of Year Sevens and shrugs. 'Maybe,' he says carelessly, then spoils the cool act by pulling a terrified face. 'They're not laughing at me, are they?'

'Laughing?' Frankie huffs. 'They're smitten. Their little hearts are racing. They think you're cute . . . so shut up and don't spoil the illusion! What is this moth-eaten jumper you're wearing?'

Kurt has topped his spindly-legged look with a huge, black, drooping handknitted jumper. It really is moth-eaten too . . . there are several darns in the wool, and one of the sleeves seems to be unravelling slightly.

'My gran knitted it,' Kurt says.

'She's a bit short-sighted, isn't she?' Frankie says. 'You could fit all three of us in there. It's practically down to your knees.'

'She didn't make it for me,' Kurt says. 'It was my dad's.'

Frankie's mouth opens, then closes again. How can you criticize a jumper that looks like a potato sack when you know it belonged to someone who died when he was barely out of his teens?

'I like it,' I tell Kurt gently. 'It's . . . different.'

'Well,' Frankie says carefully. 'It's that, all right. I suppose it has a certain quirky style of its own. Like, retro goth, maybe. I don't suppose you've ever heard of Robert Smith of The Cure?'

'The Cure were my dad's favourite band,' Kurt says.

Frankie's eyes open wide. 'Seriously?' she asks. 'Your dad liked cool music?'

'Well, yeah,' Kurt shrugs. 'He named me after Kurt Cobain of Nirvana, after all.'

'He . . . *what*?' Frankie stutters. 'Why . . . what . . . how come you never mentioned this before?'

'Does it matter?' he frowns.

I think it does matter, to Frankie. I can see her changing her picture of Kurt's long-gone parents even as I watch. Not just lentil-eating hippies with animal rights tendencies then. More lentil-eating grunge-goth fans and serious students of cool.

The bell rings for lessons, and Dan Carney, Lily Caldwell and the scally boys amble past. I know Dan acts tough and cool at school, and I try not to care. I try, but it's not quite working.

'Hey,' Dan says as he passes. It isn't much of a greeting, but it makes his friends frown. It makes Lily Caldwell frown a lot.

But it makes me smile.

Frankie McGee doesn't do PE.

'It's bad for you,' she tells me, sitting on a bench in the changing rooms while I struggle into billowing grey shorts and a shrunken white T-shirt. 'All that running around and stretching and straining. It jiggles your insides about. You could do yourself an injury.'

'It is good to run,' I tell her.

'No, Anya, that's just a rumour put about by PE teachers,' Frankie insists. 'Exercise makes you red and sweaty and out of breath. How can that be good?'

I'd like to tell Frankie that exercise keeps you fit and slim and full of energy, but I know she won't listen. She is clutching a note from her mum, excusing her from the lesson.

'What is it this week?' I ask her.

'Tummy cramps,' she says. 'Or is it migraine? I can't remember.'

Whatever it is, Miss Barlow accepts it with a resigned sigh, and Frankie gets to sit in the changing room flicking through yet another magazine while I line up with the other girls. Miss Barlow herds us out on to the school playing fields, shivering.

'It's too cold to be outside, Miss,' Lily Caldwell says. 'Can't we do something indoors?'

'Not today,' Miss Barlow says. 'I've planned a cross-country run, twice round the playing fields and through the woods. You'll run in pairs, working as a team! Choose a partner, please!'

Everyone pairs up . . . everyone except me. I'm not invisible any more and everyone is friendly enough, but they all have their own special friends.

And my friend, Frankie, is toasting her toes by the radiator inside.

On the edge of the group, I can see Lily Caldwell, arms folded, face like thunder. She has no partner, either. She doesn't really have girl friends, I realize. She's kind of a loner, when she's not with the scally boys.

Miss Barlow frowns. 'Anya, Lily, you two can go together. Keep each other out of trouble. Now, is that everyone?'

Lily scowls at me, the way she did in the cafe the other night. I feel like something slimy and disgusting that you might find under a stone.

'Follow the white markers!' Miss Barlow yells. 'I'll be timing you!'

She blows her whistle and we lurch into a jog. After two circuits of the fields, my legs are aching, my breath coming in short gasps. The runners head into the woods that skirt the school grounds, with Lily and I trailing along behind. We dodge puddles, jump ditches, clamber over fallen logs. My trainers squelch with ditchwater and there are twigs in my hair. I am beginning to think that Frankie has a point about PE lessons.

'Stuff this,' Lily says, stopping short. She looks around, then disappears off through the trees.

'Lily!' I yell. 'We are a team! Don't go!'

I push through the bushes and find her sitting on

a fallen log. She takes out a ciggy and lights it, taking a long draw.

'Lily . . . this will mean trouble!'

She looks at me, her grey eyes cold. 'Push off then,' she says. 'Like I care!'

'We are a team,' I repeat, but Lily just laughs.

'I'm not in a team with you, OK?' she says. 'Not now, not ever. I don't even like you.'

My cheeks darken. 'Why?' I ask. 'What have I done?'

Lily rolls her eyes. 'Come off it, Miss Perfect,' she snarls. 'You turn up here, all little-girl-lost, with your cute accent and your big blue eyes and your long blonde hair, fluttering your lashes, acting all shy. Well, you don't belong here, OK? You can't just barge right in and make yourself at home. Go back to where you came from!'

I bite my lip so hard I can taste blood, but I will not cry in front of Lily Caldwell. I will not.

'I cannot go back,' I say.

'How come?'

'My father has a business here,' I tell her. 'In Poland, there is nothing for us now. No home, no work, no money . . .'

'Right,' Lily sighs. 'There's nothing for you there, so you come over here and take our jobs, our homes. You get an education for free in our schools, then make friends and try to muscle in on our lads . . .'

I will never get through to Lily – she doesn't want to know. She's a bully, mean and sour and spiteful, and nothing I can do or say will ever make her like me. I wish that didn't matter, but it does, somehow.

'My father did not take the job of an English man,' I tell her. 'He gives people jobs, and my mother does a job no English person wants to do. The place we live is cold, damp, ugly. I don't want to be here, but I have no choice, Lily, OK?'

'My heart bleeds for you, Sauerkraut Girl,' she says, blowing a perfect smoke ring into the November air. 'You and your loser friends.'

I'd like to slap Lily Caldwell, wipe the smirk off her cold, cruel face, but that would make me as bad as she is. I turn, looking for the white markers, the way back to school, and I break into a run, leaving Lily behind.

Miss Barlow is not impressed. 'You were in pairs!' she tells me, as if I didn't know. 'Besides, the others were back ages ago! Where is Lily?'

Blowing smoke rings in the woods, I think, but I don't say that.

'Ridiculous!' Miss Barlow huffs. 'Didn't you understand a word I said?' She makes me stay behind and tidy up the gym cupboard, and I'm still sorting through crates of tennis balls when Lily strolls back into the changing rooms ten minutes later.

'Lily!' the teacher yells. 'Where on earth have you been?'

'Looking for *her*,' Lily says smoothly. 'She ran off and I didn't want to come back without her . . .'

'Typical,' the teacher says. 'Get changed, Lily, and run along.'

Miss Barlow walks away, and Lily flings a lazy smirk over her shoulder at me. 'One thing,' she says, and I hold her gaze steadily, a part of me still hoping for something that won't happen, for a friendship that will never be offered.

'Yes?'

'Dan Carney,' Lily says in a whisper. 'Stay away from him, OK? He's way out of your league.'

'League?' I echo, frowning. 'I don't understand . . .'

'He's mine,' says Lily. 'Hands off. Dan Carney is mine.'

16

The trouble is that Dan Carney doesn't seem to know he belongs to Lily. On Sunday morning he turns up at the flat, telling my parents he's helping me with a school project about Liverpool.

There is no school project, except in Dan's head, but his bright eyes and wide grin make up for that. He has my parents eating out of his hand. They don't know that Dan is trouble, or that he belongs to another girl. They think he's sweet, and practically bundle me into my coat in their enthusiasm to see me settling in, having fun, doing something with a friend.

We walk towards Princes Boulevard in silence.

'You're cross with me,' he says. 'What did I do?'

'You just turned up again, no warning!' I huff.

'But I promised,' Dan says. 'I said we'd explore some more! It took a while to plan, that's all. I wanted to surprise you.'

'I've had enough surprises,' I tell him. 'Sometimes I see you, sometimes not. Sometimes we are friends, sometimes not . . .'

'I thought I explained,' Dan says. 'It's complicated. My mates think I'm a hero, the teachers think I'm heading for an ASBO. I'm just juggling it all, trying to keep Mum from finding out, because that's the very last thing she needs . . .'

I bite my lip. I wish I could forget Lily Caldwell, her cold grey eyes, her perfectly painted lips blowing smoke rings into the frosty air, but I can't.

'And your girlfriend,' I ask Dan. 'What does *she* think?'

Dan stops walking. 'I don't have a girlfriend,' he says.

'Lily says you do.'

'Lily?' he echoes. 'Er . . . you've got that wrong, Anya. Lily is just a mate!'

'This is not what Lily says.'

'No way!' Dan argues. 'I've known her since primary school. I like her, sure, but . . . Lily's just one of the gang! You must have misunderstood.'

I know different. Language barrier or not, Lily made herself very clear.

Dan takes my hands, right there in the middle of the pavement. 'If I was going to ask a girl out . . . well, trust me, Anya, it wouldn't be Lily.'

My heart soars, and for a moment I don't care about Lily Caldwell. Dan likes me . . . I know he does!

'Only, it's not that simple,' Dan sighs, and the

dreams come crashing down around my feet. 'I can't ask anyone out right now, because my life's a mess and I can't keep myself out of trouble, let alone anyone else. But I like you, Anya . . . I like you a lot. When I get things sorted, well, maybe then . . .'

'Sorted?' I echo.

Dan sighs. He flops down on to a garden wall, his shoulders slumping. 'It's been a weird few months,' he says. 'Mum inherited some money from an aunt and took a lease on the cafe and the flat above. It was her dream . . .'

He frowns. 'The trouble is my dad . . . he's never around these days – and when he is, all they ever do is fight. Something's wrong, really wrong, and I don't know what to do about it. D'you know why I set fire to that book, Anya? I had to – I'd written about the rows, and Miss Matthews was going to make me read it out. She shouldn't have done that, right?'

'No,' I whisper, biting my lip. 'She shouldn't.'

Dan takes hold of my hand and squeezes it gently. 'See?' he sighs. 'Complicated.'

I can see now that complicated doesn't even start to cover it. Dan's life really is chaotic and crazy, and not in a good way.

'So . . . friends, right?' Dan asks.

'Friends,' I tell him. 'Always.'

It's not what I want, but it's better than some things. Better than the picture Lily painted, for sure. And at least now I know where I stand.

We walk on, cutting down side streets lined with towering Victorian terraces, until we come to a huge arched gateway, patterned with rich, jewel-bright colours. Dan leads me through, and suddenly we're in a busy street lined with Chinese restaurants and shops selling velvet slippers and paper lanterns bright with painted dragons. My eyes open wide.

'There's been a Chinese community in Liverpool since forever,' Dan is telling me. 'A long time, anyhow. And Afro-Caribbean, and African, and mixed race, and tons of Irish and a whole bunch of Europeans. Liverpool's a melting pot, right? The pool of life. That's what makes it so cool. We all belong . . . you, me, all of us.'

I don't feel like I belong in Liverpool, not yet. But I like the idea that I could, one day.

'Give it a chance,' Dan says, as if he can read my mind. 'It's bound to be weird at first, but it'll grow on you. It's the friendliest city in the world. I love it!'

And because Dan loves it, I want to love it too.

He has it all planned out. We take a ferry across the Mersey and back, eat cheese rolls looking out over the Albert Dock with its tall, elegant sailing ships, then mooch around the Liverpool Tate, squinting at op-art abstracts that make us go cross-eyed. Then we tour the Beatles Museum, learning all about four Liverpool boys with dodgy haircuts who just about invented pop music before developing a taste for songs about yellow submarines and marmalade skies.

Dan checks his watch. 'Shall we go?' he asks. 'I arranged a lift home, in case you were tired. Your carriage awaits . . .'

Outside, Ringo's weird yellow taxi is parked at the kerb.

'All right?' the ageing hippy grins. 'One *magical mystery tour*, coming right up. Free of charge to you two, obviously!'

It's dark by the time the yellow submarine taxi drops us off on the corner by the chippy. 'Thanks, Dan,' I say. 'Today was the best day ever.'

'Any time!' Dan leans towards me, and for a moment I think he must have changed his mind about the 'just friends' thing, but at the last minute he grins and ruffles my hair and heads off into the shadows.

I climb the steps to the flat, smiling.

The minute I push open the door to the living room, I know something's wrong. Mum, Dad and Kazia are huddled round the table, and a dull, awkward silence hangs over the room. Mum's pale face is streaked with tears, Dad's is creased and lined with worry, and even Kazia looks frightened.

Suddenly, I'm scared too.

It turns out that Dad's business partner, Yuri, has pulled out of the business and gone back to the Ukraine, leaving Dad with one big tangle of bills, debts and complaints.

'It's the recession,' Dad tries to explain. 'All across Europe, the boom times are over. Ukrainians, Poles, Latvians, all are heading home to their own countries, their families. Our workforce is half what it was. Some of the firms we worked for have folded . . . nobody knows who to trust. I'm using the last of our savings to help keep the business afloat. It's a mess. And with Yuri gone, there's only me to sort it.'

'We'll be OK, Anya,' Mum says, but I'm not sure she believes it. 'I can work extra shifts at the hotel, keep us going until things pick up.'

'What if things don't pick up?' I ask.

'If they don't . . .' Mum's voice trails away, and Dad puts his head in his hands.

'If the business fails, we have no choice,' he says. 'We must go home to Krakow.'

My heart freezes.

Not so very long ago, of course, that was all I wanted, but things are different now. Liverpool is no dream, but it's not a nightmare, either. I guess I'm starting to see the place as it really is. I'm getting the hang of the language, coping better at school, starting to settle in. And I have friends, good friends, special friends.

I don't know where home is any more, but I don't think it's Krakow.

17

Heaven's big bay window has gone all Christmassy.
Twinkling fairy lights are draped around the frames
and brightly wrapped presents are piled up in
heaps. A Christmas menu, pinned to the window,
lists mysterious new cakes with names like Santa's
Special, Rudolf's Nose and Snowdrift Slice.

'Can we try them?' my little sister Kazia breathes.

Mum is working extra shifts at the hotel, which
means that I'm taking care of Kazia after school
these days. We hang out in the flat, curled up beside
the rusty radiator doing homework, or come to the
cafe with Frankie and Kurt to take advantage of
Dan's free cake offer.

Kazia loves it, and not just because of the cake.
Dan's mum makes a big fuss of her, and she gets to
see Dan's little brothers, Ben and Nate. Ben's in her
class at school, and sometimes the three of them take
over a table and do homework together, or draw, or
read comics, or teach each other rude words in
English and Polish. Sometimes, they put on aprons

and wait on the tables, and the customers always order an extra cake or an especially fancy kind of tea, just to please them.

Today, Christmas carols are playing in the cafe and Dan is behind the counter, wearing a Santa hat.

'Now I've seen it all,' Frankie says. 'First an angel, then a saint?'

'Saint?' Dan frowns.

'Saint Nicholas,' Frankie says. 'Santa, right? No beard? No padding? No reindeer?'

'Ho, ho, ho,' says Dan. 'Very funny, Frankie.'

'We have a special day for St Nicholas, in Poland,' Kazia says. 'December the sixth. Very soon!'

'Yeah?' Dan asks.

'That's right,' I say. 'If you are good, St Nicholas will come in a sleigh with a white horse, and leave apples and gingerbread and sweets in your shoes! Not everyone does it these days, but it's a tradition in our family . . .'

'In your shoes?' he echoes. 'I've never found sweets in my shoes before!'

'That's because you are not good,' I tease. 'Bad boy!'

'I'm very good,' Dan laughs. 'Ask anyone. Well, anyone outside of school! This St Nick day sounds cool . . . like having two Christmases!'

Kazia's face clouds. 'This year is different,' she

says. 'Maybe St Nicholas won't even come. We are in Liverpool now, not Krakow. He might not find me.'

'He'll find you,' Dan says with a wink to me. 'Anya'll make sure of that. Betcha anything.'

I flop down in the window seat with Frankie while Kazia joins Ben and Nate, who are making paper snowflakes in the corner.

Dan brings us drinks and a plate piled high with the new Christmas themed cakes. 'No Kurt, today?' he asks.

'No,' Frankie says, selecting a Snowdrift Slice. 'His gran texted, telling him to come straight home. Not sure why. Wow, this cake is awesome . . . the window too! At least we know what you were doing all day, when you should have been at school. Draping fairy lights all around the window . . .'

'Mum's hoping the display will attract a few more customers,' Dan says. 'We sold three pots of tea, seven coffees, four milkshakes and thirteen cakes, yesterday. It's not enough.'

'Too right it's not,' Frankie agrees. 'How much stuff did you give away for free?'

'Er . . .'

'Exactly,' she says. 'You have to get tough. Um . . . not with us, though.'

Dan laughs and drifts back to the counter, and Ringo looms over us, alarming in his orange satin coat. 'Have you heard about the Lonely Hearts Club?'

'Beatles song, isn't it?' Frankie says.

'No, no, this is a special singles night, inspired by the song,' he explains. 'Every Friday night, starting this week, right here in Heaven. Ten-pound entry fee, to include a free cake and coffee, and Beatles songs playing all evening. All singles over the age of eighteen welcome. If you know anybody who might be interested . . .'

He offers us some flyers, printed up with swirling sixties' hearts and flowers. 'It's a tough world out there, you know.' He breaks into a random Beatles song abruptly. '*All the lonely people . . . where do they all come from?*'

I choke on my cake and struggle to keep my face straight as Ringo dances off to the next table, now singing another song at full volume. '*All you need is love . . . da da da da da . . .*'

'Yeah, right,' Frankie snorts under her breath. 'As if!'

'You don't believe in love?' I grin.

Spots of pink appear in Frankie's cheeks. 'Of course not,' she says. 'I believe in friendship.'

'What about Kurt?' I ask.

'Kurt?' she squeaks. 'Kurt Jones? Are you serious? No way! I mean, I like him, as a friend . . . but that doesn't mean we . . . erm . . . fancy each other. Or anything. Obviously.'

'Obviously,' I say, hiding a smile. 'Whatever you

say. Take a flyer for your mum, though. She's single, yes?'

'She *likes* being single,' Frankie says. 'But she also likes cake and coffee and the Beatles, so maybe . . .' Frankie folds up the flyer and slips it into her pocket.

The door chimes and Kurt bursts in, pink-faced and flustered. 'Slight problem,' he says under his breath, sliding into an empty seat. 'OK, scratch that. Major problem. Disaster, even.'

'What is it?'

He shakes his head. 'Gran was dusting on the landing when she heard a loud squeaking noise coming from my room –'

'Cheesy!' I exclaim.

'She's found him,' Kurt says. 'She opened the wardrobe and . . . well, there he was, poking his nose through the chicken wire. Gran fainted. Clean out.'

'Is she OK?' Frankie gasps.

'Yeah,' Kurt sighs. 'But I am in big trouble . . . I mean BIG trouble. Cheesy needs a new home. Like now!'

A small twitching tail appears, sticking out from Kurt's jumper sleeve. 'You can't bring him here!' Frankie hisses. 'You'll get the place closed down!'

'I know!' Kurt wails. 'I know, but I have to do something . . . can you have him, Frankie? Just for a night or two?'

'No way,' she says. 'My mum is terrified of rats!'

'Anya?'

'No pets allowed in the flat,' I shrug. 'Sorry!'

Kurt fixes his gaze on Dan. 'Hey,' he calls over. 'I've got the perfect Christmas pressie for your little brothers! A cute pet, cuddly, clever, free to good home . . .'

'Sorry,' Dan says. 'We had a guinea pig once, but we had to give it away. Ben's allergic to animal hair.' Dan's eyes open wide and he drops his voice to a whisper. 'It's not . . . the *rat*, is it?'

That's when Cheesy wriggles out of the neck of Kurt's drooping handknitted jumper and perches on his shoulder, twitching.

Somehow, we get Cheesy out of the cafe without starting a full-on riot. 'I can't believe you brought a rat into our cafe!' Dan growls. 'Are you crazy?'

But when Kurt explains how Cheesy has been turned out on to the streets just before Christmas, Dan just sighs and sends his brothers to fetch the old guinea pig cage from their attic. Half an hour later, Cheesy has a new home – a shiny, roomy cage in the corner of my bedroom.

It's a bad, bad idea, I know that, but Cheesy is homeless. And we might be too, pretty soon, if Dad's business doesn't pick up. I can't help feeling sorry for the little rat. We have a lot in common.

'He can't stay,' I remind Kurt. 'Mr Yip, the

landlord, will be angry. Just one night, until you find a proper home for him!'

'He's cute!' Kazia sighs.

'He's not staying,' I repeat. 'If my parents find him . . .'

And then we hear the door click shut, and it's too late, because Mum is home. Seven guilty faces peer at her round the bedroom door. Eight, if you count Cheesy. Caught, red-handed.

'A rat?' she says, horrified, then subsides into Polish, calling on a whole bunch of saints to save her from certain disaster.

'Gran won't have him in the house!' Kurt explains.

'My mum's terrified!' Frankie adds.

'My brother's allergic,' Dan chips in.

'But we're not,' Kazia pleads. 'So can he stay here? Please?'

'He's cooler than a guinea pig,' Ben and Nate add.

Mum shakes her head. 'No!' she says. 'He's a rat! And no pets are allowed here, anyway. And we cannot afford –'

'I'll supply food and bedding and hay,' Kurt promises. 'Think of him as a lodger. Just one or two nights, Mrs Mikalski, till I find him a permanent home . . .'

'Please, *Mama*?' I ask.

Mum rolls her eyes. 'One night,' she sighs grudgingly. 'Two at most.'

Cheesy's two nights turn into three, then four, and after that Mum stops mentioning the deadline. 'He is no trouble,' Dad comments. 'Not really. Just keep him hidden from Mr Yip!'

'He's temporary,' Mum reminds us. She doesn't add that we are too.

18

In the end, both Kazia and I set our boots out for St Nicholas on the night of December the fifth. 'Leave the boots *inside* the door,' Mum calls down. 'They'll be fine there.'

'Do you really think he'll find us?' my little sister asks. 'St Nicholas? All the way over here in Liverpool?'

'Of course!'

Kazia is not convinced. 'He might not be expecting boots, here,' she worries. 'And he might not even see them, if we leave them inside. Outside would be better, no?'

I sigh. 'OK, Kazia. He'll find them, promise, but we can leave them outside if you want to . . .' I open the door and set the two pairs of boots on the doorstep. 'There . . . all done. Come on!'

I take her hand and we run up the stairs to the living room, where Mum is waiting.

'How will he get here?' Kazia wants to know. 'There's no snow for his sleigh!'

'Shhh, Kazia. He'll come, when you are sleeping. Off to bed!'

Obediently, Kazia goes.

Dad is working late again – very late, tonight, but when we got back from school earlier, Mum was home and the flat smelt of freshly baked gingerbread. I knew she'd remembered it was St Nicholas's Day. Now Mum reaches into a drawer for a carrier bag that rustles thrillingly, rubbing her forehead with a palm. She has been getting headaches lately. I think she's working too hard.

'*Mama?*' I ask. 'Do you want me to do the boots?'

'Would you, Anya love?'

I run downstairs and open the front door a crack. The street is quiet as I press tiny red apples down into the toe of each boot, then walnuts in their shells, handfuls of wrapped sweets, and gingerbread wrapped in foil. I close the door softly, smiling as I think of Kazia finding them in the morning.

'Thank you, Anya,' Mum whispers. 'I need to sleep, that's all. Remember, I'll already be at work when you get up – I took an early shift, so I could be home this afternoon. Your dad won't be in for a while yet, so let him sleep in tomorrow. You'll take Kazia to school, won't you? There's bread and jam, so you can have toast for breakfast, something warm . . . don't be late for class!'

'We won't. *Mama*, please don't work too hard . . .'

'I'll be fine, Anya,' she promises. 'Sleep now . . . good girl.'

I awake to the sound of quiet crying, and trust me, that's not usual on St Nicholas's Day. I push back the covers and drag myself out of bed, and there is Kazia, alone at the kitchen table, sobbing her heart out. 'What is it, Kazia?' I ask. 'Whatever's wrong?'

A muffled wail leaks out. 'All . . . gone . . . wrong!' she gasps.

I put an arm round my little sister, wipe her eyes.

'What happened?' I ask again.

'St . . . St Nicholas . . .' Kazia chokes out.

'Did he forget to come?' I frown. Perhaps some passing drunk has helped himself to the sweets? Maybe Mum was right. We should have left the boots inside the door.

'It's worse,' Kazia whispers. 'Much worse. No apples, no gingerbread, no sweets . . .'

She tugs my hand, pulls me down the stairs and out on to the step. 'No nothing!' she wails, and finally the penny drops.

I sink down on to the doorstep, dismayed.

Some lowlife loser has gone and nicked our boots.

I suppose most girls have three or four pairs of boots and shoes. Some, like Lily Caldwell, probably have dozens. But Kazia and I, we have just one pair each. Oops – make that no pairs now.

117

Kazia grew out of her summer shoes before we flew to Liverpool, and my ballerina flats were so worn and scuffed I didn't bother to pack them. I knew my boots would take me through the first few weeks of school and after that, I imagined, there would be any amount of new shoes and boots, new everything, if we felt like it.

It didn't quite work out that way.

And now our boots have been stolen, or kidnapped by the milkman, or kicked around the streets and chucked into Princes Park boating lake by drunks coming home in the early hours.

Leaving boots on the doorstep on the night of December the fifth in Liverpool is clearly not a good idea.

And now we have no shoes.

'Should we wake Dad?' Kazia asks, but telling Dad is the very last thing I want to do – he has enough on his mind. As for Mum, well, maybe she left before the boots were taken this morning, or perhaps she just didn't notice at all.

Either way, it's my fault – Mum told me to leave the boots inside the door, and I listened to Kazia and left them outside. Now they're gone, and all because of me.

'We won't tell Dad, or *Mama*, OK?' I tell Kazia. 'Not yet. I'll think of something, I promise!'

So Kazia pulls on her black canvas PE pumps,

and I have to wear my fluffy slippers, at least until I get to school and drag the trainers out from my locker. Great. I have never been so ashamed in my whole, entire life.

I time it carefully, so that the bell is just ringing as we arrive at Kazia's primary, but still, I get a whole bunch of smart comments on the way.

'Oi, girl, yer feet's all hairy!'

'That the new fashion, or what?'

By the time I get to St Peter and Paul's, I'm running late, and I'm so mortified I'd like to crawl under a stone and stay there for the rest of the day. I kick off the fluffy slippers at the door and stuff them into my satchel, then sign in late at the desk and head for my locker, padding in my stockinged feet along deserted corridors draped with drooping paper chains.

'Forgotten something?'

Dan Carney is sitting on the bench outside Mr Fisher's office, grinning. 'Like your shoes, maybe? Or is it a tradition that Polish girls go barefoot on December the sixth, in thanks for the sweets St Nicholas left them the night before?'

'No,' I tell him. 'It's not a tradition.'

Dan tips his head to one side, baffled. 'So . . .?'

I sink down on to the bench beside Dan. 'We put our boots out last night, me and Kazia,' I confess. 'And I filled them with sweets and cake and fruit . . .'

'Was Kazia pleased?'

I sigh. 'Not exactly. Our boots are stolen. No shoes for me or Kazia today, and no sweets, for sure.'

'You're kidding?' Dan asks, outraged. 'Nicked? That's low. That's very low. And . . . you've got no other shoes for school? Seriously?'

I open my satchel just enough to show a fringe of pink fluff.

'Ah,' says Dan. 'My favourites. Well, don't let Fisher see them. He is not in a good mood. I was cheeky in class, plus I owe him three homeworks, so now I have to do my lessons here, so Fisher can supervise. This school gets more like a prison every day. I don't know why I bother to stick around, half the time.'

'You don't,' I say, with a sad smile. 'Half the time.'

Dan just shrugs and grins. 'Well, can you blame me? Seriously, Anya, what'll you do about the boots? Will you be OK?'

I bite my lip and tilt my chin up, trying for a smile. I'd like to tell Dan about what's happening with the business, ask him for a hug, but I remember that he doesn't want a girlfriend, and if he did it wouldn't be a girl with no boots, no future, a girl whose life is falling apart.

I am the last thing Dan needs. Maybe he'd be better off with Lily after all?

'Stuff this,' Dan growls, getting to his feet. 'Life's

too short for biology notes and being polite to Fisher. I'm going to fix this, Anya.'

He pulls on a beanie, winds a stripy scarf round his neck, and throws me a big grin. 'See you later, OK?'

'Dan, you can't just go –'

'Watch me,' he says.

He walks down the corridor, pushes through the double doors and breaks into a sprint just as the school secretaries run out, yelling, to try and stop him.

Mr Fisher's door creaks open.

'Was that Dan Carney?' he barks at me. 'Where is he? What's going on? Did you see him?'

'Sorry,' I say, smiling sweetly. 'I don't understand . . .'

19

Frankie wants to know why I'm wearing white trainers with black tights. 'It's an unusual look,' she says. 'I'm all for unusual, Anya, but this is a little bit . . . weird.'

'It's a long story,' I sigh.

We're in art, making decorations for the school Christmas dance. Mr Finlay's art room is a mess of tinsel, glitter and glue.

'I want an ice palace theme,' Mr Finlay announces. 'Think icicles and snowflakes . . . and perhaps a giant papier-mâché snowman, filled with sweets and presents?'

You can tell that Mr Finlay once dreamt of a career in children's TV, or designing sets and costumes for the theatre. Teaching art to sulky teenagers was probably not what he had in mind. A roll of chicken wire appears, newspapers are torn into confetti shreds and buckets of thick, gloopy paste are sloshed around until the art room looks like a war zone.

'Nice shoes,' Lily calls over to me. She is avoiding

the chicken wire and glue, and seems to be making herself a miniskirt out of silver tinsel. 'All the rage in Poland, that look, is it?'

'Ignore her,' Frankie says. 'You can wear dodgy trainers if you want to. It's a free country.'

'I've lost my boots,' I confess.

'How do you lose a pair of boots?' Frankie asks. 'And supposing you do, why not just wear shoes instead?'

I bite my lip.

'You *do* have shoes, right?' Frankie says. 'You don't just have one pair of boots to your name?'

'I have trainers,' I say brightly. 'And pink fluffy slippers.'

'You're joking?'

Kurt unwinds a roll of cellophane, ready for us to slice into silvery streamers. It's kind of like my life, unravelling, coming apart in my hands. I know one thing for sure. Staying quiet about this is no longer an option.

'At home, money is tight,' I say. 'Dad's business is in trouble. Big trouble. We might have to go back to Krakow.'

'No way,' Frankie says. 'Tell her, Kurt!'

'No way,' Kurt echoes. 'Things can't be that bad!'

'Worse,' I tell him. 'We have no money, and Mum and Dad are working late every day. It feels bad . . . like there's a black cloud following me the whole time. And now, Kazia and I have lost our boots . . . and we have nothing else!'

'Sheesh. That's why you're always looking after Kazia these days. Why didn't you say something?'

Because I didn't want pity? Didn't want even to think about it? I can't answer that.

'This is pointless,' Frankie says, throwing down her scissors. 'Anya's in real trouble, and we're making streamers? Why bother? People like us never go to the Christmas dance, anyway.'

'Maybe we should,' Kurt says. 'It might be Anya's first and last Christmas here. Shouldn't we make it one to remember?'

Frankie's eyes shine. 'We could,' she says. 'Why not? I never really had anyone I could go with, last year, but . . . well, we could dress up, stick together, have a laugh! What do you think, Anya?'

'I guess . . .'

'It might take your mind off things,' Frankie says. 'Forget your troubles for a while. Forget about Dan Carney too. He is so not good enough for you, Anya. Did you hear about this morning? He was on report, outside Mr Fisher's office, and he just stood up and walked out of school! Everyone says he's going to be excluded again. That boy is crazy!'

'Dan's OK,' I argue. After all, he walked out of school because of me, didn't he? I can't exactly explain that to Frankie, though. Where Dan is concerned, she just can't see the attraction. She'd probably accuse him of heading off to shoplift me a pair of flash shoes to replace the missing boots.

'I just don't think he's right for you.'

'Isn't that up to Anya and Dan to decide?' Kurt says loyally. 'You can't choose who you fall for, right?' He shoots Frankie a loaded look, but typically, she doesn't even notice.

'Dan and I are just friends,' I sigh. 'And that's all we'll ever be, now it looks like we're going back to Poland.'

Frankie shrugs. 'I was just saying. Anyway, who needs boys, right, when you've got good friends? The three of us can stick together, go to the dance as mates . . .'

Frankie seems not to notice that Kurt is a boy, and worse than that, a boy with a crush on her. She barges on, oblivious.

'We'll have fun, dress up, have a laugh . . . isn't that what Christmas is all about?'

I'm not sure what Christmas is all about, not at St Peter and Paul's, anyhow. Across the classroom, the chicken-wire snowman is taking shape, plastered with torn newspaper, dripping with paste. Mr Finlay unveils a huge blanket of cotton wool to make the final layer. It's kind of scary.

Frankie spots a tube of black acrylic paint by the sink.

'Don't worry about the whole Poland thing, OK, Anya?' she says. 'We can sort this. We're your friends, and we won't let this happen. As for the trainers . . . well, they're easily fixed.'

She squeezes out a curl of black paint and hands us each a brush, and slowly the scabby white trainers turn into scabby black ones. With silver marker-pen stars, courtesy of Frankie.

'See?' she says. 'They're actually quite cool.'

As long as I don't go out in the rain, anyway.

'Something might turn up, y'know,' Kurt says. 'Strange things happen all the time.'

'You're not kidding,' Frankie says. 'Last night was the first meeting of the Lonely Hearts Club at Heaven . . . and Mum went! I only gave her the flyer as a joke, really, but she went, and she had a great time. She got chatted up by a really nice bloke, and now she's saying that maybe she got it wrong all these years, and not all men are trouble. Incredible, right?'

'Sounds like,' I agree.

'So don't give up, Anya,' Frankie says. 'Things will work out, they always do.'

The bell rings for the end of the lesson, and Mr Finlay blinks in surprise as the kids stream past him, out of the door. His hair is stiff with paste, his fingers covered with cotton-wool fluff, his classroom looking like the scene of a small massacre.

'Trust me,' Frankie says, as we pick our way

through the puddles of glue. 'Kurt is good at plans. He'll work it out. No worries.'

Kurt doesn't look quite so confident. I'm not sure his plans are brilliant enough to overthrow a global credit crunch, rescue Dad's business and find me new shoes by teatime, but I guess you never know.

I pick Kazia up from school, wearing my handpainted trainers with the silver stars. They don't attract quite as many comments as the pink fluffy slippers, which is kind of a relief.

'What will we tell Mum and Dad?' Kazia wants to know.

I haven't quite figured that one out. Maybe they just won't see? They're so tired these days they probably wouldn't notice if Kazia and I were wearing red stilettos.

It's dusk by the time we cross the road towards the chippy, and I don't see them at first, the boots sitting neatly on the doorstep of the flat. It's only when Kazia starts to whoop and yell, when she lets go of my hand and sprints ahead to see, that I realize what has happened.

They're not our boots, of course. That would be too much of a miracle, but they're boots, and that's pretty amazing. Kazia's are pink suede with a sheepskin lining and pink flowers stitched on the sides. Mine are black with a turn-down cuff, like little pixie boots. Both are the right size, and both are stuffed with tangerines and sweets and topped with a gingerbread man wrapped in cellophane.

'He came!' Kazia is squealing. 'There was no snow, and maybe we were in a different place, but he found us! Maybe a day late, but who cares? And it doesn't matter about the old boots, because now we have new ones, much better ones!'

I look over to the corner, frowning, as a movement catches my eye. I'm almost sure I can see a shadowy figure with unruly braids and angel wings, disappearing into the shadows.

20

Dan used his savings to buy the boots, cut-price, from the discount shoe shop in town. He said it was an early Christmas present.

Mum noticed that the boots were different, but Kazia insisted that we found them on the doorstep on St Nicholas's Day, and I think Mum was just too tired to question it. Besides, we had boots, new boots, and that was the main thing.

Dan had another trick up his sleeve too. 'It's a treat,' he explained. 'For Kazia, really. Friday evening, OK?'

How do you say no to a boy like Dan Carney? You don't. It's Friday evening and I'm ankle deep in snow, watching Kazia chatting to a fat old man with a bushy white beard who is sitting beside her in a sleigh piled high with presents.

He's Santa Claus, the British version of St Nicholas, and we're outside his workshop at the North Pole, Dan, Ben, Nate, Kazia and me. How cool is that?

OK, it's not really the North Pole. It's a converted shop in town, with life-size models of reindeer and fairy lights and Christmas music playing, but it's half-price on a Friday night, so here we are. Dan explained the whole thing to Mum, and she said it sounded great and gave us money for tickets and bus fares. 'Can we afford it?' I asked, anxious.

'Anya, it's Christmas,' she sighed. 'I won't let every penny I earn be eaten up by your dad's business. You and Kazia need a treat.'

So here we are, standing in the snow, and there are real elves and fairies, and Santa himself, sitting on a plush red-velvet seat in a sleigh that's strung with silver bells.

It's not real snow, of course, just a kind of glittery powder that catches the light and crunches a little when you walk on it. The elves may not be real elves. One of them is chewing gum, and another is listening to an iPod, but they are wearing pointy green hats and red boots and wrinkly green tights. The fairies look bored, and one of them has a pierced eyebrow and a ladder in her tights, so I'm pretty sure they're not real either. I think they could be students, earning a little extra cash, and that's OK.

It's even possible that the man in the red suit and white beard may not be the real Santa Claus, but his blue eyes are kind. He listens very patiently to Kazia as she talks. There is a long queue of hopeful children, including Ben and Nate, but Santa doesn't rush things. Perhaps Kazia is telling him the story of the stolen boots, or explaining about Dad's business and the flat with peeling wallpaper.

Santa hands her a gift from the sack beside him, a painted Russian doll, which opens up to reveal a whole family of smaller dolls inside. Kazia gives him a big hug, and one of the bored-looking fairies has to drag her away with a wave of her wand and a sprinkle of fairy dust. Everyone in the queue smiles and sighs and the elves look at their watches. It's obvious they can't wait for it to be eight o'clock when the whole late-night grotto thing is over.

'Oh, Anya!' my little sister says, her smile as bright as the fairy lights. 'He says he will bring us everything we want, on Christmas Eve night!'

I catch Dan's eye. Kazia will probably be getting an apple and a selection box and a pair of new mitts on Christmas Eve night, if she's lucky. Still, right now she's happy, and Ben and Nate are too, asking Santa for PlayStation games and bikes and rollerblades, and pulling on his beard gently, to check it's the real deal.

'I gave Santa one of the vouchers, Dan,' Ben announces as we walk back up Renshaw Street afterwards. 'For the free cakes. I told him to come any time. Think how many customers we'd get if the real Father Christmas started hanging out in our cafe!'

'Great idea,' Dan says.

'Maybe the elves and fairies will come too?' Nate smirks.

I smile. That's all the cafe needs . . . a whole bunch of grumpy elves and fairies, alongside Ringo with his yellow cab and Lonely Hearts Club. Oh, and the misfit schoolkids too.

Kazia, Ben and Nate are still fizzing with excitement, skipping on ahead, the boys playing with the plastic swords they got from Santa while Kazia dances around them, bright-eyed, laughing.

'It was a very kind thing,' I tell Dan. 'Taking Kazia to see Santa. It was very different from Poland, but good!'

'Mum used to take me, when I was a kid,' he shrugs. 'I loved it, and Ben and Nate still do. Mum's too busy this year, and it's not like Dad's gonna help, so I promised . . . and I had an idea Kazia might like it. I didn't want her to think that Liverpool was just full of boot thieves!'

'She doesn't,' I promise him. 'She loves it – we all do.'

What would Dan think if he knew we might be heading back to Krakow in the New Year? I can't even bring myself to tell him, because it would mean facing up to it myself. What if Dan didn't care? And worse – what if he really, really did?

We reach the bus stop and lean against the shelter.

The Christmas lights flicker and shine, and the streets are busy with groups of office workers on Christmas nights out. Restaurants and bars are overflowing, and every second person has fluffy reindeer antlers or a length of tinsel round their neck. Kazia, Ben and Nate link arms and start some random carol singing, and a group of women fuss and sigh and give them a five-pound note.

'I was wondering . . .' Dan says. 'You know the Christmas dance Frankie and Kurt have been talking about? On the last day of term? I just thought I'd ask . . . um . . . d'you think we should go? Me . . . and you?'

I can't stop grinning. Dan wants to go to the Christmas dance – with me! The whole evening feels like magic, with the Christmas lights shimmering, the office workers with their Santa hats, the kids singing.

And then the whole thing skids out of shape.

'I'd like that,' I start to say, but Dan isn't listening any more.

He's miles away, his face startled, shocked, angry. I can hear Kazia, still singing 'Jingle Bells' and getting most of the words muddled up, but Ben and Nate are silent, staring, mouths open.

I follow their gaze.

A tall, dark-skinned man in a smart suit is coming out of the bar just along from the bus stop, a fair-haired woman in a skimpy red party dress draped around his neck and whispering into his hair. The man is laughing, but the grin dies on his lips as his gaze slides over Ben, Nate and Dan.

'Hello, Dad,' Dan says.

Ben and Nate just blink, shocked and silent, and Dan turns and walks away. It's left to me to grab Ben and Nate by the hand and run along after Dan, with Kazia in tow and Dan's dad chasing us along the street.

'Dan! Ben! Nate!' he shouts. 'Hold on! I can explain! It's not the way it looks!'

Dan stops and turns to face his dad, who is standing a few feet away, raking a hand through fuzzy black hair in a gesture I've seen Dan use a million times.

I gather the kids in behind Dan.

'You're a liar,' he spits out. 'A rotten, lousy liar!'

'Dan, son, you don't understand –' the man says.

'We understand, all right,' Dan says, his voice shaking a little as he speaks. 'We've heard the rows, seen Mum crying. We've known for months that something was going on, so please don't pretend you can explain. It's pretty clear already, from where I'm standing.'

'But, son –'

'Don't call me that!' Dan bites out. 'Because you know what? You sure don't act like a dad!'

I don't know what to do, but Ben is clinging to me, tears welling in his big brown eyes, while Nate and Kazia just look shell-shocked. I don't know how to help, but I know I need to get the kids out of here, get Dan away too. A number 80 bus slides to a halt beside us with a squeal of brakes, and I herd the kids on board. 'Come on, Dan,' I tell him. 'Please?'

Dan jumps on, looking back over his shoulder. 'You know what?' he yells. 'I hate you, even if you are my dad. I hate you, and I'll never, ever forgive you for this! So why don't you just get lost, leave us alone? We don't need you! We don't want you!'

The doors slide shut and the bus lurches away from the kerb.

Mum is making honey cakes, and the flat is filled with the rich, sweet smell of them baking. For the first time in weeks, she isn't working weekend shifts at the hotel. 'We'll have a proper Sunday,' she says. 'I can't keep going at this pace, and nor can Jozef. So today we'll have some family time, a good, Polish dinner and then Mass at the cathedral with our Polish friends.'

'Where is Dad?' Kazia frowns. My little sister looks tired too – her cheeks are pink and her eyes are huge and shadowed. I think Mum's right. We all need some family time, some chill-out time.

'Jozef will be back soon,' Mum says. 'With a special surprise . . .'

After Friday night, when Dan, Ben and Nate saw their dad with another woman, it seems especially important that my family, at least, are together today. I don't think I ever realized before how fragile a family can be.

I don't know what happened on Friday after

Dan, Nate and Ben got home, but I don't think it was good. I held Dan's hand tightly all the way home on the bus. I could feel him hurting, and Ben and Nate too.

Kazia and I went along to the cafe first thing on Saturday, but the sign said *closed*, and Ringo was on the doorstep, wondering aloud what might have happened. I wondered too.

'Girls, don't look so sad,' Mum says now, lifting the honey cakes out of the oven and setting them down to cool. 'No use worrying. Come, both of you, and see what arrived in yesterday's post . . .'

She brings out a large parcel, layered with brown paper and decorated with Polish stamps and postmarks.

'It's Gran's writing!' I say. 'For us!'

'Christmas presents!' Kazia squeals.

We tear off the brown paper to reveal a cardboard box filled with scrunched-up newspaper, packed in tight, as if to protect something. Mum fishes two small presents out from the packing, wrapped in red crêpe paper and tied with ribbons, one labelled for me, one for Kazia.

'We haven't even got a tree to put them under,' Kazia sighs. 'What else is in there?'

Mum lifts out the last of the packaging, and Kazia's eyes grow round.

'The Christmas castle!' she breathes.

Inside the box is the old tin castle Dad made years ago in Krakow when I was little. It's a szopka castle, traditional to Krakow, with turrets and towers and little domed roofs, intricate and beautiful. The tin has been shaped and scored and patterned, the whole thing painted with bright, rich colours.

Every year in Krakow, there's a competition to see who can create the best design, and back when I was three years old, Dad won the prize. He never entered again, but we took the castle out every December and sat it in the window with candles burning beside it, to show that Christmas was coming.

'It brings us luck,' Dad used to say.

We couldn't take it to Liverpool, of course. It was too bulky to pack, and besides, other things were more important. We gave it to Gran and Grandad, and now they've sent it over to us, just in time for Christmas – and just when we really, really need the luck.

Kazia and I carry it to the window, and set it on the rickety side table there. It looks beautiful.

In the bottom of the box, a silver star made of beaten tin glints brightly. 'The star!' I grin. Again, made by Dad back in the days when he had time to cut and shape and pattern things from tin or wood, the star sits at the top of the Christmas tree every year, watching over us all. There is something comforting about having our old things around us, even in this dump.

'But no tree . . .' Kazia sighs, and right then the door swings open and Dad comes in, a Christmas tree slung over his shoulder.

'No tree?' he echoes. 'This is the best tree in the city, especially for my girls!'

'Oh, Dad!' Kazia grins. 'It's perfect!'

Well, not quite – it's slightly lopsided and kind of bare and brown-looking all down one side, but we wedge it into a bucket and edge it into a corner so that you can't see the brown bits. Mum switches on the radio and finds some Christmas songs, then we cut stars from white paper and make apple and orange slices to dry out on the radiator and string together with nuts and sweets, the way we used to back in Krakow. Dad lifts Kazia up to fix the star on top, and finally I can see that this is the best Christmas tree in Liverpool after all.

'Have you seen the Christmas castle?' I ask Dad. 'Gran and Grandad sent it over in a big parcel, so now we'll have all the luck we need . . .'

Dad frowns, as if he doesn't believe in luck any more, and I know he is thinking of happier times, times in Krakow when the castle glinted bright in the wintry sunlight and silent snow. Even I can see that it looks out of place here, perched on a lopsided table next to the draughty, grey window.

'Maybe,' Dad says. 'But right now, what we need is some of your mother's stew with dumplings and rye bread, then honey cakes to sweeten us up.'

'I'm not hungry,' Kazia complains. 'I'm all tired and hot and achey.' Mum rests a palm against my little sister's forehead.

'You're very warm,' she says. 'And clammy. You don't look well at all. I hope you're not sickening for something, Kazia.'

She makes my little sister a nest of blankets on the threadbare sofa, settling her against the cushions with lemon squash and a warm honey cake. In minutes, Kazia's head droops and she is sleeping, one blonde curl sticking damply to her cheek.

'Oh dear,' Dad sighs. 'I was hoping we could eat and then take a walk up to the cathedral . . . catch up with our Polish friends. Perhaps one of them might help with the business? A small loan, perhaps, just to tide us over?'

Most of Dad's contacts from the Polish Mass at the cathedral are struggling as much as we are, but I don't say that. If Dad is desperate enough to be asking acquaintances for a loan, things must be bad.

'Well, we'll eat, anyway,' Mum says. 'Perhaps Kazia just needs a rest?'

Mum is dishing out stew and dumplings when the doorbell rings. It's Dan. He looks even worse than Kazia, as though he's been up all night, and maybe the night before that too. He's forgotten to put on a jacket, and his eyes seem shadowed, dull.

'He's gone,' Dan blurts out. 'This morning. He packed his bags and moved out, to be with *her*. My dad's gone, Anya . . . and it's all my fault!'

It doesn't matter how many times we tell Dan he's not to blame – he's just not listening. 'If I hadn't got angry,' he argues. 'If I hadn't yelled and told him to get lost . . .'

'You were upset,' I tell him. 'Anyone would be angry, Dan.'

'I made everything worse,' he sighs. 'I always do. I should have told Ben and Nate to stay quiet, forget what we saw. Maybe then things wouldn't have gone crazy?'

Dan is sitting at the table with us, staring down into his stew.

'I don't think so,' Dad says. 'Keeping quiet wouldn't have made this go away. Sooner or later, the truth always comes out.'

'I'm worried about Mum,' Dan says. 'She didn't open the cafe yesterday, but today she was down there before nine, even though it's a Sunday. She opened up and a couple of people wandered in, but it's no use. She's acting crazy. She took all of the presents out of the window display and dumped them into the wheely bin out back, pulled down the tinsel and the lights. It's a mess. And now she keeps putting sad songs on the CD player and crying into the cake mix . . .'

'I see,' Dad frowns. 'That is not good.'

'She needs a friend,' Mum says briskly, clearing away the dishes. 'She has been so good to Anya and Kazia, making them welcome at the cafe after school. Now she needs our support in return.'

Mum wraps some honey cakes in foil and takes her coat from the rack. 'I will go and see her,' Mum says. 'Tell her to be strong. She can get through this.'

Dad reaches for his coat. 'I suppose we can see our Polish friends another day,' he sighs. 'Kazia's not well enough for Mass, anyway.'

So Dan takes Mum and Dad over to the cafe, and Mass at the cathedral – and the chance for Dad to ask his friends for help with the business – is shelved. I stay in with Kazia. She is still sleeping an hour later, when Dad comes back in and scoops up the Christmas castle.

'I thought I'd let Dan's mum borrow it, for the window display,' he explains. 'I've cleared up the mess and rigged up some new fairy lights, and this will make a great centrepiece. And, of course, it brings good luck . . .'

'But, Dad!' I argue. 'What about us? Don't we need all the luck we can get?'

'It's just a loan,' Dad promises. 'It will be back in

time for Christmas. And besides . . . you can't give luck away. The more you pass on, the more you get back again.'

I really hope he's right.

It turns out Kazia has flu. She's off school all week, curled up on the sofa in a swirl of blankets with Cheesy snuggled in beside her. I get into the habit of coming straight home to sit with her, reading her stories from my old storybooks, about smugglers and spies and buried treasure.

'Britain isn't really the way it sounds in the stories,' Kazia sighs. 'It's still cool, though!'

'Yes, it's still cool.'

'It's not fair, being ill in the last week of term,' she says. 'I'm missing all the fun stuff! The nativity play, the party, the presents! What if my friends forget me?'

'They won't forget you,' I promise. 'They'll still be there in the New Year.'

I'm not sure if *we* will be here in the New Year, but I don't tell Kazia that. I've heard Mum and Dad talking late at night, and I know things are bad . . . very bad.

'At least you won't miss the Christmas dance,' my

sister chatters on. 'You'll be the prettiest one there, and on the stroke of midnight Dan will ask you to dance, but if you run away and lose your pixie boots, you'll never get to be a real princess.'

I laugh. 'I think you're getting the story muddled up a bit,' I tell her. 'Besides, I have no idea if Dan will even be there – he hasn't been in school all week. And trust me, I'm not planning to lose my boots again!'

'You haven't even got a fairy godmother,' Kazia frowns.

I roll my eyes. 'Ah,' I tell my little sister. 'Now that's where you're wrong . . .'

'You shall go to the ball!' Frankie says. 'Seriously, Anya. Take a look!'

I'm at Frankie's, getting ready for the Christmas dance. I'd like to say I spent hours searching my wardrobe for something to wear, but it was more like minutes. I picked out the only thing I owned that might do, a blue print dress with a fitted top, gathered sleeves and a short, sticky-out skirt. Frankie did my make-up. She even straightened my hair and sprayed it with something, and now she is steering me towards the mirror.

I blink. The girl in the mirror looks a little like me . . . but better. The dress, which seemed plain and little-girlish back in Krakow, is somehow cute and cool with borrowed turquoise tights and flat boots. My hair is long and blonde and sleek, with a sheen of glitter where the light catches it, and Frankie has outlined my eyes and stroked sparkly blue shadow across my lids.

'It's great!' I tell her.

'How about me?' Frankie demands. 'Think I'll make an impression?'

Only a blind man would be able to miss Frankie tonight. She's wearing a black minidress with a red-and-black tutu skirt, red stripy tights and Doc Marten boots. Her hair has been crimped and backcombed until it looks like she just crawled out of a hedge. 'Does my bum look big in this?' she asks, looking backwards over her shoulder into the mirror. 'OK, don't answer that, Anya. My bum looks big in everything.'

'You look cool,' I promise. 'I wonder . . . will Dan be there, tonight, do you think?'

'Dan?' Frankie raises an eyebrow. 'I dunno. He's missed so much school lately. He'd be crazy to show his face with all those teachers around . . . Fisher's out to get him. Like I said, Anya, he's no angel . . .'

'We're just friends,' I say.

'Yeah, right!' Frankie smirks.

I blink. 'OK,' I say. 'I do like Dan. Is that a crime? I've tried not to, but I can't help it. I know he's trouble, but I like him a lot, and I think he likes me

146

too. And anyway, Frankie, you're not exactly an expert when it comes to the whole crush thing, are you?'

'What's that supposed to mean?'

'It means that Kurt is crazy about you, and you haven't even noticed! The boy of your dreams is right there under your nose, Frankie – open your eyes!'

'Boy of my dreams? Kurt Jones?' Frankie echoes. 'No way. Kurt is only interested in beansprouts, biology homework and the square root of 73.5. He doesn't have a romantic bone in his body.'

'Are you sure about that?' I say.

'Trust me, Anya, I'm sure,' Frankie says, blotting her crimson lipstick and grabbing her coat. 'C'mon, let's go!'

You wouldn't think St Peter and Paul's could ever look magical, but tonight it does. The darkness hides the worst of the peeling paint and the graffiti, and someone has draped fairy lights all around the main entrance. Frost glimmers on the path as we approach.

A gang of girls dressed up in satin prom dresses and tinsel headdresses totter past us, giggling, and then we see Kurt, waiting for us on the steps. He looks like his own version of smart, in black skinny jeans, a collarless white shirt and a big, sagging jacket that looks like it came from a jumble sale.

'Hey!' he yells. I wink at Frankie, and I'm almost sure I see her blush as Kurt links our arms and the three of us go inside.

The school hall has been transformed. Lit only by fairy lights, it is shadowy and mysterious, the ceiling hung with rustling streamers, silver tinsel and hundreds of glitter-edged snowflakes. The scary snowman we made in art has been shunted into a corner behind the refreshments table, where Mr Fisher and Miss Matthews are serving lemonade and mince pies.

Mr Critchley, dressed in a Santa suit, is on stage running the disco, and already a sea of excited Year Sevens are jiggling about on the dance floor while the Year Eights stand around the edges, trying to decide when it would be cool to join in.

I can see Lily Caldwell across the hall, risking frostbite in a red-sequinned minidress, and Dan's bad-boy gang lounging carelessly against the stage, trying to talk Mr Critchley into playing Jay-Z instead of corny Christmas songs. I can't see Dan, though, not anywhere.

Kurt, Frankie and I load up on mince pies and lemonade and start making our way back through the crush of kids, when someone grabs at my waist, and there's Dan, in angel wings, laughing as he whirls me round.

'Hey, guys!' he yells above the music. 'Nice jacket,

Kurt. Love the tutu, Frankie! And, Anya . . . you look awesome. Seriously.'

'You came!' I grin.

'We agreed, didn't we? I even wore the angel wings for you . . . well, it *is* Christmas! Is Fisher here?' Dan looks around anxiously. 'He's one person I do NOT want to see tonight. I'm in serious trouble, and it's all his fault . . .'

'What happened?' I ask.

'What didn't?' Dan scowls. 'Fisher is one sad, power-crazed loser, right?'

'Right,' Kurt says, blinking. 'And he's over by the refreshments table right now with a ladle in his hand, Dan, so you'd better be careful . . .'

'Thanks, mate.' Dan frowns. 'C'mon, Anya. Nowhere's safe.'

He takes my hand and pulls me after him through the crowds, out into the darkened corridors.

23

It's not easy to find a quiet place to talk, but Dan leads me into the cloakrooms and we sit among the coats and jackets, side by side in the half-light.

'It was always gonna happen,' Dan huffs. 'Fisher's been on my case for ages, and he went crazy when I legged it out of school the other week. He's been sending letters and leaving messages on the answer phone. I've been sneaking home while Mum's at work to bin the letters and erase the messages. But we came home from the cafe a bit earlier than usual today. The phone was ringing, and Mum got to it before me . . .'

'Mr Fisher,' I finish. 'Oh, Dan.'

'It's a disaster, Anya,' he groans. 'Mum knows all about the skiving off now. I've told her a whole raft of lies over the last few months . . . no wonder she's mad. And, of course, Fisher told her about the fire thing and how I was suspended for three days when she just thought I had the flu . . . Anya, what am I gonna do?'

'It's a mess,' I admit. 'What did your mum say?'

Dan winces. 'She was just so . . . so *angry* with me,' he says. 'I've never seen her like that before. She kept saying that I'd let her down, that she'd never been so disappointed in me. That hurt, Anya. I was doing it all for her! She'd never have managed otherwise!'

I bite my lip.

'You think I was wrong too, don't you?' he says. 'But I had no choice! Mum and Dad had big plans for the cafe – catering for parties, a delivery service. But none of that fancy extra stuff ever got off the ground, and Mum could barely keep the place afloat. When Dad walked out . . . well, what else was I supposed to do? I had to help, didn't I?'

Dan rolls his soft brown eyes up to the ceiling.

'I've really messed up,' he sighs. 'Fisher's gonna involve the authorities. Mum might get fined, or worse. She's furious. Ben started crying and Nate said I'd spoiled Christmas, and I . . .' Dan puts his head in his hands. 'I said that I hated the lot of them, and I slammed out of the house. I've gone and made everything about a million times worse.'

Dan takes my hands and holds them tight. 'I wish you could understand,' he whispers. 'I wish you just knew how it feels when your life is falling apart . . .'

I bite my lip. 'I do know, Dan,' I tell him. 'Not about the parents thing, but . . . well, things are pretty awful for me too. I've been trying to tell you for weeks, but I didn't know how . . . and I know this isn't exactly a good time, but if I don't do it now I might not get another chance.'

I take a deep breath. 'Dad's business is failing. Unless we get some kind of a miracle, it looks like we'll be heading back to Krakow in the New Year.'

Dan's eyes flash with anger. 'Krakow? No way! They can't do that – you can't do that, Anya! I need you, OK? I need you here!'

'I'm sorry,' I whisper. 'I didn't know you'd care . . .'

Dan rakes a hand through his dark braids. 'You didn't know I'd care?' he echoes. 'Are you crazy? Oh, Anya, what a mess . . . we've wasted so much time! We have to be together, OK, we have to! I know I'm not good enough for you, I know things are complicated, but . . . well, nobody understands me like you do, OK? Nobody.'

His eyes shine in the half-light.

'What if we run away, Anya?' he breathes. 'You and me? We could be together, away from all this junk. Your parents can't make you go back to Krakow then, and Mum will see how much she needs me, and Dad will be sorry and maybe come back home . . .'

For a moment I can almost see it, me and Dan, together, running, laughing, with nothing to pull us apart. Then the image slides out of shape, dissolving like snow in the sunshine.

'No, Dan,' I whisper. 'We can't. It'd just hurt everyone even more. Running away is not the answer.' I pull Dan to his feet. 'We have to face things. Put things right, bit by bit. And you have to talk to Mr Fisher – tell him you need one more chance.'

'He hates me,' Dan argues. 'He'd never listen, and all the teachers think I'm no good.'

'I know different,' I say. 'I know a boy who helps his family, is kind to strangers, makes magic out of nothing for his friends.'

Dan looks at me for a long moment, his dark eyes burning.

'Sometimes, it feels like you're the only one who ever sees the good in me,' he says.

He leans towards me, so close I can feel the warmth of his breath on my cheek, the tickle of his braids as they fall against my face. My eyes flicker shut, and my heart is hammering so loud in my chest I swear the whole school can hear it.

Then some Year Sevens blunder along, looking for their coats, and we spring apart, wide-eyed, guilty.

Dan rolls his eyes up to the ceiling. 'Typical,' he says.

I grin, hiding my blushes behind a curtain of hair.

'Come on,' I tell him, pulling him to his feet. 'We will find Mr Fisher, put this right. You can change, Dan – work hard in school, make your mum proud. No more trouble.'

'I can't talk to Fisher!' Dan protests. 'Not in front of everyone! I won't know what to say!'

'Speak from the heart,' I tell him. 'Say the things you said to me. Say sorry.'

'Sorry?' Dan pulls a face. 'Do I have to?'

'Yes, you have to.'

'And what about you, about going back to Krakow?' Dan asks.

I sigh. 'Some things you just can't fight,' I tell him. 'No matter how much you want to. But still, I'm hoping for a miracle!'

We walk into the hall, into the half-light of frosted snowflakes and tinsel streamers. The dance floor is packed now, and Mr Critchley is dancing around on stage as he lines up the CDs and sets the disco lights flashing. I see Lily Caldwell dancing with a circle of Dan's bad-boy friends around her. She's moving in a bored, listless kind of way, waving a sprig of mistletoe around and wiggling her bum a lot. Then her eyes swoop over Dan and me, and her eyes harden, her mouth forming a thin, cold line. Well, I have more important things to worry about than Lily.

'There's Mr Fisher, over by the drinks –'

'I can't talk to him there!' Dan yells into my ear. 'Not in this racket! Anya, he'll never listen.'

'He'll listen,' I promise. 'Stay here, Dan, I'll fetch him. You can talk outside, beside the coats, like we did. Please, Dan?'

'I guess,' Dan agrees.

By the time I battle my way through the crush of kids to get to the refreshments table, Mr Critchley has changed the CD and a slow, slushy number floods the room. Kids sprint off the dance floor in a panic, but I see Frankie and Kurt, hand in hand, walking up to dance, and I smile. Looks like things are finally working out for them too.

It takes forever to get Mr Fisher to understand. 'Someone needs to talk to you,' I yell at him, over the mince pies. 'There's a pupil in trouble. It is important, serious, you must come now!' Mr Fisher straightens his tie and follows me across the hall.

There's just one problem . . . Dan is not standing by the door, where I left him. There's no sign of him at all.

'Who did you say needs to speak to me?' Mr Fisher frowns. 'What's this all about?'

I look around the hall, and then I see him, and

my heart turns to ice. Dan is in the middle of the dance floor, with Lily Caldwell, dancing. As I watch, Lily leans in, waving the sprig of mistletoe over Dan's head, and kisses him full on the lips.

24

I don't notice anything after that. I push past Mr Fisher, shove my way through to the cloakroom, grab my coat. And then I'm outside, running across concrete that glints with frost, down towards the school gates.

'Anya!'

I don't want to hear anything he has to say. What's the point? It's all lies, I know that now. I was kidding myself all along.

It's not as if people didn't warn me. Frankie told me to be careful, Lily warned me off – even Dan himself admitted he was trouble, right from day one. I thought I knew better. I believed in Dan . . . that was my big mistake.

'Anya! Wait! I can explain!'

He's behind me, his feet slapping against the concrete as we reach the gate. He catches hold of my sleeve and I spin round to face him, furious.

'It wasn't the way it looked!' he says, and I think of another night, in town with Dan, Ben, Nate and

Kazia, when a man with dark skin and slanting cheekbones said exactly those words.

I didn't believe them then, either.

'Anya, please, it meant nothing . . .'

My breath comes in burning gasps, and my cheeks are streaked with tears. 'It meant something to me,' I tell him, and my hand flies out to drag a handful of white feathers from the angel wings. I want to hurt Dan, the way he's hurt me. 'Some angel you are. Leave me alone, Dan. You . . . you're just like your dad!'

Dan's eyes widen, and he opens his mouth to protest, but nothing comes out. His eyes harden and his face shuts down, and he shrugs off the feathered wings and lets them fall to the ground. Then he turns and walks away from me, and I'm glad.

I never want to see him again.

It's just past ten when I get back to the flat. Kazia, on the mend now, is sitting at the table with Mum and Dad, eating toast made from Tesco Value bread.

Mum looks up, alarmed. 'Anya?' she asks. 'We didn't expect you back for another hour. Is everything all right?'

I've wiped the tears away, tried to tidy my make-up, but when I catch a glimpse of my reflection in the mirror on the wall, I can see I look windswept and weary and sad.

'The music was rubbish,' I tell them. 'We left early.'

Well, Dan and I did, anyhow. We just didn't leave together.

'But it was your special night!' Mum argues.

'I know . . . I just wasn't in the mood. Besides, it's Christmas Eve tomorrow. I wanted to be home.'

I sit down at the table, take a piece of toast. The bread is not as nice as the rye bread Mum makes, but it's cheaper than buying the ingredients to bake it. I scrape a knife round the empty jam jar, then go to the cupboard to see if there's any more. It's almost empty. A jar of sauerkraut, an apple, half a bag of flour. No jam, no honey.

'I'll shop tomorrow,' Mum promises. 'We'll still have our special meal tomorrow night. Traditional. We'll make things as nice as we can, even though . . .'

She looks at Dad, and he looks at the tabletop guiltily.

'I have to go into work in the morning, just for a little while,' he says. 'I have a few things to do, but don't worry, this is the last time. Things will change now.'

'So business is better?' I ask.

Dad looks uncomfortable.

'Tell them, Jozef,' Mum says gently.

'Not better,' Dad says. 'I've tried and tried, but ever since Yuri left things have been getting worse and worse. Problems, debts, complaints . . . I can't make it work. My savings are gone . . . it's time to stop. Tomorrow I'll clear the office. The business is over.'

Kazia flings her arms round Dad. 'Never mind, *Tata*!' she says. 'It's almost Christmas Eve. Maybe Santa'll bring you a new job? I asked him to fix everything up, and he said he'd see what he could do.'

I blink. So that's what took Kazia so long at the grotto. She wasn't asking for dolls and games and sweets, she was asking for a miracle. How do you explain to a seven-year-old that there are some things Santa just can't fix?

Dad tries. 'Kazia, I wish it could be that simple.'

I haven't forgotten what Dad said would happen if the business failed. How could I?

Mum sighs. 'It's good news really, girls,' she says brightly. 'No more nasty flat, no more struggles with the language. Things just haven't worked out for us here. We're going home, back to Krakow.'

Kazia pulls away. 'No!' she says. 'I like it here! I like school, and my friends, my teacher. I'm the best in my class at art, Miss Green says!'

'Oh, Kazia,' Dad says. 'I'm sorry. We cannot stay. No jobs, and no money . . . not even enough for rent, for food. It's all gone.'

'Gran and Grandad are sending us money for air

fares,' Mum explains. 'We'll have the cheque by New Year, maybe sooner, and we'll go right away. We can stay with them until we get back on our feet, find a flat of our own . . .'

'No!' Kazia argues. 'We can't! I want to go back to school. How will I see my friends, say goodbye to them?'

'We'll be gone before the term starts,' Dad says. 'It's better this way.'

'Do we have to go?' I plead. 'Kazia and I, we're settled at school. We have friends. Our English gets better every day.'

'I'm sorry, Anya,' Dad says. 'We have no choice.'

No choice. Kids have no choice, kids like me and Kazia, uprooted and brought halfway across Europe to start from scratch because Dad had a dream. And now that the dream has crashed, we will be uprooted again, torn away from our new friends and taken back to where we started from. Are we supposed to pick up our old life again, three months on, as though nothing has come in between?

If I'd listened to Dan . . . we could be running now, away from Liverpool, from peeling wallpaper and stolen boots and cheap white bread with no butter or jam. But I didn't listen, and I should be glad, because Dan let me down, trampled all over my heart and walked away into the night.

Maybe it's just as well I'm going back to Krakow?

I don't believe that, though, not for a moment. Even with Dan out of the picture, Liverpool is where I want to be . . . it was my dream too, after all. I want to stay, work on my English, be with my friends, see whether the picture-postcard cottage with the roses around the door actually exists.

I want to stay.

'I asked Santa!' Kazia argues. 'St Nicholas! He promised, and I have been good, very good, so definitely he will fix it! You'll see!'

I can't sleep. An hour ago, Kazia crawled into bed with me, her face wet with tears. Her arms twined around me and we stayed that way, me stroking her hair, until she drifted into sleep.

Three months ago, I was packing to come to Liverpool, full of hopes and dreams that fizzled and died in the relentless British drizzle. I hated Liverpool at first, but that was before I got to know it. Now I can see that it has a crumbling kind of beauty, a chaotic warmth, a crazy, quirky heart, and I will miss it. I'll miss Frankie and Kurt too. I will even miss Dan.

My mind slips back to the dance, replaying those scenes, those words. Dan Carney . . . and Lily Caldwell. It doesn't make sense. It's like the worst ever betrayal, the sharpest cut. I got Dan so, so wrong, but still, I'll miss him. I'll miss him and I will never, ever forget him.

I wish I hadn't told Dan that he was like his dad. I saw his face crumple with hurt, and for a split second I was glad. Now, though, I'm not so sure. Hurting someone who has hurt you doesn't make you feel better. Sometimes, it makes you feel worse.

Kazia stirs and stretches, and I sigh, my heart dull and heavy in my chest, my eyes dry and aching with unshed tears. Somewhere around two o'clock, I think I hear a bicycle bell outside, and I run to the window.

There's nobody there, of course.

25

I must have fallen asleep eventually, because when I wake it's past nine. I hear Dad shout goodbye, that he'll be back later, and the front door clicks. The day looks overcast and heavy, the way I feel.

I roll out from under the covers, taking refuge in the bathroom to shower and dress. Slowly, I wash away the sparkly make-up from last night, the glitter from my hair. I wish it was as easy to wash away the taste of disappointment.

The doorbell rings, and my heart leaps.

Maybe Dan woke feeling the same way I do? I'm not sure what kind of explanation could make me feel better now, but if he tried, that would be something. And at least we could say goodbye . . .

'Anya!' Mum is calling. 'Are you up?'

I slick on some eyeliner and go through, but it's not Dan, it's his mum. Ben and Nate are squashed up on the sofa with Kazia, watching a cutesy Christmas film, and Karen Carney is sitting at the table in the little kitchenette, her eyes shadowed, scared.

'Have you seen him?' she asks, and my heart sinks down to my boots. 'Have you seen Dan? We had a row yesterday, and he slammed out of the house and he hasn't been back. All night! I'm worried sick.'

I swallow. 'Dan . . . he was at the school dance, last night,' I say. 'We talked, and then . . . well, we had a row too. Dan walked away. I haven't seen him since.'

'What time was this?' Mum asks.

'Ten to ten, maybe?' I say.

'Why hasn't he been home?' Karen wails. 'I'm worried sick! What if he's run away? I said such terrible things to him, and I know he's a good boy really. If he was in trouble at school, it was my fault. I've been so wrapped up with the cafe, for months and months now . . .'

I feel cold all over. Running away . . . isn't that exactly what Dan planned to do?

Mum puts an arm round Karen's shoulders. 'Don't blame yourself,' she says. 'You do your best for your boys, the best you can.'

'But it wasn't good enough,' Dan's mum sighs. 'Dan was off school such a lot – there was always a school trip he wasn't going on, or a toothache, or a headache that wore off as fast as it started. I should have known they were excuses. I should have known he was truanting!'

165

'Dan wanted to help,' I try to explain. 'He wanted to be there for you.'

'I know,' Karen says. 'And I let him. I didn't ask too many questions because I didn't want to know the answers. And now he's disappeared . . .'

I bite my lip. 'Mrs Carney,' I say, and everyone turns to look at me. 'Last night – well, Dan was talking about running away. I told him it wasn't a good idea, but . . .'

Mum blinks. 'Could he have gone to see his dad maybe?'

'That's not possible,' Mrs Carney whispers. 'James is in Manchester, staying with . . . with his . . . his friend.'

'We should check,' Mum says gently. 'Do you have a mobile number for Dan's dad?'

I sit on the edge of the sofa, shaky and sad. I remember the things Dan said last night, about his dad, about wanting to see him, talk to him. I remember the two of us yelling in the dark. I told Dan he was exactly like his dad, and watched his face fall. My stomach churns with guilt, thick and sour and sickly.

If anyone made Dan run away, it was me.

'James?' Mrs Carney is saying. 'It's me. Is Dan there? He hasn't been home, and I wondered if . . . well, if he could be with you?'

I sneak a look at Karen Carney, and watch her

face fall. Dan is obviously not at his dad's, and a prickle of fear slides down my spine. So where is he?

'James, what shall I do?' Karen whispers, her voice cracking as the tears begin. 'It's all my fault. Anything could have happened to him! Oh, God . . . I'd better call the police!'

She lets the phone slide from her fingers.

Mum puts her arms round Karen Carney the way she does with Kazia and me when we're tired or sad or sick. 'Be strong,' she says gently. 'Dan needs you to be brave. You must go to the police, and then take the boys home, wait there, in case Dan turns up, or calls. The police will do everything they can, Karen, and if there's anything we can help with . . .'

Karen Carney wipes a blur of tears from her tired eyes. 'No, no, you've done enough,' she whispers. 'Unless . . . the cafe. I don't suppose . . .?'

Mum smiles. 'Of course,' she says. 'It's Christmas Eve. It could be a busy day for the cafe, and the last thing we need is another business folding around here, right? We will keep the place running until Dan is found. I promise.'

Heaven is the busiest I've ever seen it. Every table is full of shoppers sipping hot chocolate or steaming lattes, eating cake, laughing. There's no way Mum, Kazia and I can cope with this alone, so I call

Frankie, tell her Dan is missing. She's here within five minutes, Kurt in tow, with hugs and a can-do attitude.

'I'm sorry, Anya,' she tells me. 'I know I've always said Dan is trouble, but only because I didn't want you to get hurt. You know I like him really, right? I hope he's OK . . .'

'He'll turn up,' Kurt tells me. 'The police will find him. Try not to worry.'

'I'm not,' I whisper, but my voice cracks dangerously and I have to turn away before my eyes mist and blur.

Frankie and Kurt work flat out all morning, taking orders and waiting on tables. Even Ringo has been dragged from his corner to help. Like Frankie's mum, he met someone special at the Lonely Hearts Club, and he's been floating around, all starry-eyed, ever since. He's singing – Beatles songs, of course – as he wipes the tabletops and stacks the dishwasher.

Me, I fill out the orders and make the drinks and try hard to keep the fear and guilt about Dan from swamping me.

The sweet, spicy smell of Christmas fills the cafe as Mum bakes batches of honey cakes and spiced gingerbread, with Kazia as her assistant. The CD plays carols on a loop and every customer seems happy. It'd almost be fun, if it weren't for the worry gnawing away at my heart. I try not to think about Lily or the kiss or Dan's angel wings lying trampled on the frosty ground.

It's safer not to.

26

'What happened to you at the dance last night, anyway?' Frankie asks, slapping down one scribbled order for cake and coffee on to the counter. 'You disappeared, left me on my lonesome with Kurt . . . and now Dan's done a runner.' Frankie's face clouds. 'Hang on, have I missed something here?'

I sigh. 'I had a big row with Dan,' I admit. 'I thought we were getting on OK . . . getting closer, maybe. And then I saw him kissing Lily Caldwell.'

'You saw *her* kissing *him*, you mean,' Kurt scoffs, dumping a tray of piled-up plates and mugs on the counter. 'Lily was threatening everyone with that sprig of mistletoe. I bet she couldn't wait to corner him!'

I frown. 'What do you mean?'

'If someone asks you for a kiss and there's mistletoe around, you can't say no,' he explains. 'It's an old Christmas tradition. Don't you have that one in Poland?'

I blink. 'I'm not sure . . . Maybe . . .' I whisper.

Kurt shrugs. 'Dan probably didn't stand a

chance.' He takes a freshly loaded tray from me and heads back out into the crowd.

I think back to the dance, to the moment I saw Dan and Lily, her arms locked round his neck. Could Dan have been backing away slightly? Maybe it wasn't quite what it seemed?

I frown. 'But . . . but . . . he didn't exactly struggle.'

Frankie raises an eyebrow. 'Anya,' she says patiently. 'He's a *boy*. When a girl comes at them with mistletoe, they kiss first and think later. There were a lot of mistletoe kisses last night. You can't take them too seriously. You know I've had my doubts about you and Dan,' Frankie says. 'But . . . well, you can't really blame him for this. Lily's always fancied him, and whatever you saw, I bet it was pretty one-sided. It's not like they got together or anything – at the end of the night, Lily was in the girls' loos, crying. Her mascara was all down her cheeks, and she said she was through with boys. They were all rats, she said.'

Relief floods through me, followed by a dawning dismay. It looks like I jumped to the wrong conclusion – and that makes the things I said to Dan even worse. I lashed out, wanting to hurt him. And I guess I succeeded.

Guilt churns in my stomach, mixed up with fear. Where is Dan? If he was headed for his dad's place, wouldn't he be there by now? I glance at the clock. It's just past one. Dan has been missing too long. It's fifteen hours since I last saw him – since anyone last saw him.

'Hey,' Frankie says softly, sliding an arm round my shoulders. 'Chin up, honey. Dan's a big boy. He can look after himself. Things will work out.'

'I hope so.'

'I bet he goes to his dad's,' she says. 'Try not to worry, Anya.'

Kurt hurries up to the counter again, balancing a fresh tray of piled-up crockery while delivering yet another order for cakes and coffee. Frankie winks at me. 'Face it,' she grins. 'Whatever Lily reckons, I'd say rats are smarter than boys. Possibly better looking, too . . .'

'Watch it,' Kurt laughs, flicking her with a dishcloth. 'Did she tell you, Anya? About us?'

'Hang on!' Frankie says. 'I'm getting to it. Thing is, last night . . . after you vanished, we were stuck with each other. We got talking, and then we danced, and then . . .'

'She asked me out,' Kurt says.

'You asked me!' Frankie insists.

'She did,' Kurt repeats. 'And I said maybe, but she's kind of determined, so I guess there's no escape . . .'

I dredge up a grin. 'Finally!' I tell them. 'It's

about time! I am glad for you, really. You make a great couple.'

'Sorry to interrupt, kids,' Ringo says, looming up to clear away the trays of dirty crockery. 'But we've got a busy cafe here, guys. People are waiting for their orders!'

I sigh and start setting out the trays, and Frankie and Kurt head back into the fray. The tips bowl beside the till fills up, is emptied and fills up again. Five or six people are huddled beside the cafe door, waiting to be seated. There has never been a queue here before, that's for certain.

The cupcakes, meringues and cream slices are selling fast, and even Mum's freshly baked honey cakes and gingerbread are dwindling. In the kitchen, two of Mum's big Christmas cakes, rich with fruit and spices, are cooling on a rack, ready to be iced, and she's mixing up a sponge cake batter when the cafe door opens with a jingle and Karen Carney rushes in, with Ben and Nate behind her.

My stomach lurches. I want to ask about Dan, but my tongue is dry as dust, tangled in my mouth. The tray I'm loading with milkshakes and meringues slides out of my hands and on to the floor. Silence settles over the busy cafe, and Ringo has to rush forward with a mop to clear up the mess.

Mum comes out of the kitchen, Kazia behind her.

'Have they found him?' she asks. 'What's happening? Have they found Dan?'

Karen Carney just smiles and nods and falls into Mum's arms. 'He's safe,' she says into the silence. 'He's at his dad's. The police are there right now, and James has promised to bring him home as soon as everything is sorted. Dan's safe!'

A few customers look puzzled, but someone in the corner starts to clap and pretty soon the whole place is cheering and yelling out 'Happy Christmas'. Dan is safe – he may not care about me any more, he may not be speaking to me, but still, he's safe. I take a deep breath in and my body starts to relax for the first time in hours.

'You see?' Frankie says to me. 'Told you he'd be OK! You worry too much!' Kurt just grins and puts an arm round my shoulders, squeezing gently.

Karen Carney has tied on an apron and bustled into the kitchen. 'I'll never be able to thank you, Klaudia, for what you've done,' she says. 'Oh . . . those cakes look amazing! Shall I ice them, do you think?'

'No, no, everything's under control,' Mum assures her. 'We can manage. Sit down, I will make you some tea . . .'

Dan's mum laughs. 'Thanks, Klaudia, but I need to keep busy – until James brings Dan back home,

174

anyway. You've all been fantastic, but please, let me help!'

When Mum ices a cake, she just blankets it with a layer of sweet, white icing and adds a ribbon round the sides. When Dan's mum does it, it's a work of art. On one, she piles white icing up round the edges like drifts of snow, with a perfect white snowflake piped on top, delicate as lace, dusted with silver. On the other she moulds a leaping reindeer, pulling a sleigh piled high with bright, beautiful 3-D presents.

'They are beautiful,' Mum breathes. 'You have a real talent, Karen. It's a shame we didn't make more – I thought we'd sell them in slices, but these I think we could sell whole, to take away . . .'

As I slide the cakes in behind the display counter, an elderly woman, paying for her order, opens her eyes wide. 'Those cakes are wonderful!' she murmurs. 'I've never seen anything like them! I was planning to get a Christmas cake from the supermarket, but . . . well, I don't suppose I could have one of these?'

Ringo grins. 'You could indeed. These cakes are handbaked, packed with fruit and spices, and individually iced by a true artist. You won't get anything like them, anywhere in the city!'

'How much are they?' the elderly lady asks.

'I'll just check . . .' I go through to the kitchen to ask.

'What do you think?' Karen Carney frowns. 'Is ten pounds too much?'

'Not enough!' Mum says. 'We could charge fifteen, twenty maybe!'

But when I go back through to the counter, it's too late – Ringo has opened his mouth and put his foot in it. 'They're twenty-five pounds each,' he tells the woman, and my heart sinks. Who pays twenty-five pounds for a cake, especially in the middle of a recession? Ringo doesn't seem to care. 'They're artisan cakes, each one unique,' he blusters on. 'Baked to a secret family recipe, hand-iced . . . a real one-off, luxury product.'

'I'll take the reindeer one,' the woman says.

Ringo smiles as he lifts it into a cake box and ties it up with a flourish of curly ribbon. Half an hour later, the snowflake cake has sold too, to a young woman. 'I'm getting married in April,' she explains. 'It's not a big wedding, but I want it to be special. Personal. Do you make wedding cakes to order?'

Karen Carney blinks. 'Wedding cakes?' she echoes. 'Yes, yes, we can do that!' Karen scribbles her name and phone number on to the cake box, and the woman thanks her and leaves smiling.

'Wow!' Dan's mum says. 'Fifty pounds for two cakes – and all thanks to you, Klaudia!'

'For a wedding cake, you could charge a hundred and fifty pounds, two hundred maybe,' Mum points out. 'That is where the big money is. People will always spend on special occasions, one-off events.'

'A couple of orders like that in a week would keep us going,' Karen agrees. 'I could make little frosted cupcakes as wedding favours too. I'd never have managed without you today – all of you! Keeping the cafe open was the very last thing on my mind, yet we've probably taken more money than ever before . . .'

'No worries,' Ringo says.

'We were glad to help,' Kurt adds. 'Payback time for all the free cakes!'

'It's nothing,' Mum shrugs. 'Just like the bakery back in Krakow, but much more fun!'

'You worked in a bakery?' Karen blinks.

'It'll be back to the bakery soon,' Mum says. 'If they will have me. The last few weeks have been very bad for Jozef's business. It's all over for us in Liverpool.'

'Oh, Klaudia, no!' Karen says.

'You can't go!' Frankie bursts in. 'That's just not fair! Anya doesn't want to go!' She drags a hand across her eyes, leaving a trail of smudged eyeliner.

'There is nothing to be done,' Mum sighs. 'I am sorry, Frankie. We all are. But now . . . well, there are no options left to us. Come, Anya, Kazia – we should be getting back. We have a meal to prepare . . .'

'We'll never forget you, Anya,' Frankie says. 'We're friends forever, right? The three of us.'

My friends fold me up in a three-way hug, and that's bad, because suddenly my throat aches and my eyes sting and I think I might cry.

Karen hugs Mum too. 'Thanks for today,' she says. 'You've been a real friend. And I'm sorry, so sorry, about Krakow.' She presses a cake box into Mum's hands, a £20 note tucked under the ribbon.

'No, no . . .' Mum protests, so Karen hands the cake box to me, and Mum doesn't argue any more.

Just as we're getting our hats and scarves on, the door jingles and an old man comes in. He's small and round, with rosy cheeks and a bushy white beard, and the minute Kazia sees him her face lights up. 'It's Santa!' she squeals. 'From the grotto!'

'Oh, Kazia, it's just a nice gentleman,' Mum hushes her, but when I look again at the old man I wonder if Kazia is right. He looks very familiar, and didn't Ben give the Santa from the grotto a voucher for free cakes?

Then again, I guess that every plump old bearded guy gets mistaken for Santa at this time of year.

'Come on, girls,' Mum says. 'It's Christmas Eve! What are we waiting for?'

We step out into the cold air just as the first flakes of snow begin to fall.

27

Back in Poland, Christmas Eve is the main part of the Christmas celebrations. We have our own traditions, our own style of doing things, and it doesn't involve turkey or chocolate yule log or stockings hung over the fireplace. It's just as well, as we can't afford turkey or yule log, and we don't have a fireplace, just radiators that cough and splutter and rattle in the night.

It doesn't matter – we like it our way.

Mum dives into the supermarket on Aigburth Road, stocking up on basics, spending the extra £20. Then we go home, the snow falling softly around us as we walk.

Dad is there already. 'It's finished,' he tells Mum quietly. 'The office is tidy now, the keys handed in. All over.'

'Oh, Jozef,' she sighs, and the two of them hug for a long moment. I see Dad's eyes shine with tears and I have to look away.

'I've spoken to Mr Yip,' Dad goes on, and his

voice is creaky and strange, as if he doesn't quite trust it to hold out. 'Told him the rent situation. When the money comes from your mum and dad, Klaudia, we'll pay him. I promised. Even before the air tickets. He's a reasonable man – he'll wait. He wished us happier times ahead.'

'There will be,' Mum sighs. 'There have to be.'

'Hey, hey,' Dad grins then, and his voice is strong and bright and brisk again, and the shine in his eyes is just that, a shine, nothing more. 'It's Christmas Eve! Everything starts fresh tonight . . . we'll put old troubles behind us! Girls, have you looked closely at the tree?'

Beneath the thick green branches, a clutch of brightly wrapped parcels have appeared – presents! Kazia pounces on them, grinning. 'This one's for you, Anya . . .' She hands me one that's kind of shoebox-shaped. I start to smile, imagining red shoes, sparkly shoes, shiny, pretty shoes. Oh, I wish!

'So . . . one present, each, to unwrap?' Dad says. 'Nothing will spoil our Christmas Eve, hey, girls?'

Kazia goes straight for the biggest parcel, tearing at the paper, and I open mine. Sure enough, there are shoes . . . not red or sparkly or spike-heeled, but soft black suede with little heels and delicate ankle straps. Perfect.

'I love them!' I tell Mum and Dad.

Kazia's present, though, takes my breath away.

It's a wooden dolls' house, painted in glossy red and white with pink roses climbing up the walls. It's exactly like the house I once imagined we'd live in, but in miniature.

'It's beautiful!' Kazia breathes, her eyes wide. 'You see? Santa knew!'

I think that the dolls' house might have more to do with Dad. He made me a Noah's Ark when I was small, with tiny carved figures of Noah and his wife and two of every kind of animal I could think of. Even after he went away, he'd carve and paint animals and send them to Kazia and me, obscure animals we'd never even thought of, like buffalo, racoons, llamas.

The dolls' house, though, that's something else. It must have taken months to make, with a front wall that opens up to reveal the rooms inside, each one painted and carpeted and fitted with tiny tables, chairs and beds.

I imagine Dad working on the house, secretly, at the office. I imagine him painting little red window frames and shading in the roof tiles, adding in the climbing roses curling up the shiny white walls, and then coming home to this sad little flat above the chippy. When Dad decided to make a dolls' house for Kazia, he clearly had no plans to go back to Krakow. I imagine packing the dolls' house up with bubble wrap and cardboard, ready to ship to Poland. It's going to be kind of awkward.

Mum is preparing food for the Christmas Eve feast: beetroot soup with mushroom dumplings, herring in sour cream, spiced cabbage and flat, golden wafer bread. She opens up the cake box Karen gave her to reveal a chocolate layer cake drizzled with runny white frosting.

'So kind,' Mum smiles. 'I will miss Karen. Kazia, Anya, will you set the table? The cloth's in the drawer, candles too.'

Kazia runs to get them, the big white cloth we've used for Christmas Eve ever since I can remember, and the box of cheap white candles from the local supermarket. We had red candles back in Krakow, tall, twisty ones, but this year we can make do.

I push the sofa back against the wall and Kazia and I drag the kitchen table out into the centre of the living room, so we can take our time and stay warm while we feast. It's traditional to sprinkle a little hay underneath the cloth to remind us of the stable, so Kazia borrows some from the bag Kurt brought for Cheesy. We smooth the cloth over the top, arrange the candles on saucers and set five places for people to eat.

There is always an extra place at the table on Christmas Eve, in case an unexpected visitor arrives. It brings good luck, and it's a ritual we never forget, although guests are rare on Christmas Eve in Poland. It's a family time, and of course our family are far away in Krakow – Gran, Grandad, Uncle Zarek, Aunt Petra. Still, traditions count.

Darkness is falling as Mum sets out the food, an odd number of dishes for luck. Usually there are thirteen dishes, but this year money is tight and it's only five. I can't help thinking that the table looks bare and empty compared to last year, when every space was filled with bowls and platters heaped with rich, steaming, festive food. There's no point, though, in thinking that way, today of all days.

'Any sign yet?' Dad calls.

'Not yet . . .' Kazia is stationed at the window, looking out for the first star of the evening. As the youngest child, this is her special task. I remember when it was my job . . . I'd be at the window the moment dusk threatened, watching so hard, willing the sky to darken, longing to see the first bright star of Christmas.

In Liverpool, the sky has a dull orange glow and it's snowing steadily now. Spotting the lamp post across the street will be a challenge, let alone the first star, but suddenly Kazia whoops, jumping up and down. 'I saw it, I saw it!' she insists. 'I saw the Christmas star!'

That's all we need for the feast to begin, and Mum lights the candles and Dad breaks the golden wafer bread and reminds us that now all grudges will be put behind us, all troubles are over. Dad is dishing out beetroot soup and dumplings when the doorbell rings.

'Who is this?' Mum asks. 'At this time . . .?'

Dad is on his feet.

'Unexpected guest,' he says, and goes to see who it could be.

28

There are seven dishes on the table now. Our landlord, Mr Yip, worried after Dad's visit earlier, has brought some deep-fried sausage and chips up for us.

'Christmas is a special time,' he says. 'I don't celebrate it myself, but I know what the spirit of Christmas is all about. I won't have you going hungry at this time of year. As for the rent, I've talked it through with the wife. There'll be no rent due this month, none at all. Didn't you fix the broken window and mend the kitchen cupboard, put new shelves up in the bathroom?'

Dad smiles. 'Thank you, Mr Yip,' he says simply. 'You have no idea how much that means. Please, stay with us this evening, share our meal, help us to celebrate Christmas.'

'Thought you'd never ask,' Mr Yip grins.

Mum is dishing up herring with chips on the side when the doorbell rings again. She blinks, setting an extra place at the table hastily just as Dad opens the door.

'Tomasz! Stefan!' Two young men shuffle in, stamping the snow from their boots, talking in Polish. They clap Dad on the back and set vodka, fruit and chocolates down on the table. They are two of Dad's best workers, loyal to the end.

'You paid us every week, even though we knew it came from your own pocket,' Tomasz says. 'We're grateful.'

'We know what it's like to be far from home at Christmas,' Stefan adds. 'We wanted to wish you a Happy Christmas, and a prosperous New Year . . .'

Before they can sit down, the doorbell rings again. 'Who now?' Dad puzzles. 'So many visitors!'

Mum ushers Karen Carney into the room, her coat starred with snow. She is carrying Dad's Christmas castle with its shining towers and bright painted patterns, still draped with Christmas lights from its stay in Heaven's big bay window. I'm glad to see Karen, really I am, but I can't help wishing Dan was with her.

'You said it would bring good luck, and I truly think it did,' she says, setting the castle down beside the window. 'I thought it was important to make sure it was back where it belongs for Christmas, with all of you . . .'

Mum plugs in the fairy lights and the whole thing

glimmers brightly in the darkened room. 'It's lovely,' she smiles. 'Thank you for bringing it back, Karen. Please join us . . . all of you! Eat! Enjoy!'

The meal has turned into a kind of buffet, with everyone crowding around, filling their plates, eating with forks and spoons and teaspoons, mixing chips with spiced cabbage and deep-fried sausage with mushroom dumplings.

'Dan is home!' Karen tells us, in between mouthfuls. 'James brought him back an hour ago. We talked and talked, all of us together, cleared the air a little. James won't be coming back, but that's for the best, I can see that now. And me and Dan . . . well, we'll be OK.'

'Where is he?' I dare to ask.

'He fell asleep, right there on the sofa – he had no sleep at all last night, and he must have walked twenty miles today, looking for his dad's place. He was worn out. He doesn't know, Anya, about you going back to Krakow. I'll tell him in the morning. He'll be very upset, I know. But right now he needs to rest, and James is staying a while to spend some time with Ben and Nate, so I thought I'd call over and thank you all properly for today.'

I'm glad, of course, that Dan is home. I'm glad he is sleeping, curled up on the sofa with his dad nearby. But I wish he was here, I really, really do, even if it's just to say goodbye.

'I'm sorry you're leaving,' Karen is saying. 'I know, Jozef, how hard it is to keep a business afloat at a time like this. I know that you don't really *want* to go back to Krakow, and I had an idea –'

'An idea?' Dad frowns.

'Klaudia, you could come to work at the cafe!' Karen suggests. 'You could help me make designer cakes for birthdays and weddings! I couldn't pay as much as the hotel, but we could build the business together . . .'

Mum's eyes shine. 'We're a good team,' she says.

Dad clears his throat. 'Karen, it's a wonderful offer,' he says. 'But it's not enough. We've lost everything, there's nothing left. I've spoken to my old boss in Krakow, and he will find a place for me in the team, even after all this time. I have to take it.'

'Jozef was a joiner,' Mum explains. 'A real craftsman.'

'I can see that from the szopka castle,' Karen nods. 'There was an old bloke in the cafe this afternoon, asking about that . . .'

'Really?' Dad asks, surprised. 'Still, I could never sell it, it's special to our family. Now . . . let's put all of that aside, yes? It's Christmas Eve! I for one would like a slice of this wonderful chocolate cake . . .'

The party breaks up after ten. There are hugs and Happy Christmas wishes and then, as soon as they appeared, our visitors are gone.

'We have more friends here than we know,' Mum says, her eyes soft and misty. 'So kind, so unexpected . . .'

'It will be hard to leave these good people,' Dad agrees. 'But I don't see any other way.'

And the doorbell rings again.

Mum looks at the table, a wasteground of empty bowls and dishes, with barely a crumb of food left. 'There's nothing left to offer!' she panics. Dad puts an arm round her, and I move to clear the dishes, so it's Kazia who walks over and opens the door.

'Oh!' she says. 'It's you! I thought you'd never get here!' She leads an elderly man with a bushy white beard into the room.

'You see?' Kazia is saying. 'I told you he'd come! It's Santa! He'll fix everything!'

Dad steps forward, frowning. 'Sorry . . . have we met?'

The old man smiles, and I realize he does look familiar – he's the old guy Kazia mistook for Santa in the cafe earlier.

'Not yet,' he says to Dad. 'I have met your charming daughter before, though I didn't realize . . . down at the grotto in town . . .' He drops his voice to a whisper, so that Kazia can't hear. 'Their regular Santa had a flu bug, and I stepped in at the last minute as a favour to a friend.'

I blink. It *is* Santa – or the closest we're going to

get, anyhow. The old man from the cafe and the fat old guy in the red suit surrounded by grumpy elves . . . they're one and the same. Kazia isn't as crazy as I thought.

'See?' she's saying. 'See?'

'I know it's Christmas Eve,' the man goes on. 'I do apologize. I planned to wait until after the celebrations, but I'm not a patient man. It's hard to be patient, at my age. I couldn't resist coming along, just to see you, just to ask . . .'

'See who?' Dad says. 'I think there must be some mistake . . .'

'No mistake,' the old man says, his eyes drifting to the window where the castle twinkles and shines. 'I am looking for the man who created that! I enquired in the cafe this afternoon – I saw your wonderful szopka castle in the window. I've never seen one in this country before. I asked at the counter, and the lovely lady explained who you were, told me where you lived . . .'

'Ah,' Dad says. 'Karen mentioned that. I'm sorry, it's been a wasted journey, the castle is not for sale . . .'

'No, no . . .' The old man strokes his beard, peering at the szopka. 'I don't want to buy it. I was wondering if you have any others, if making things . . . toys, decorations . . . is something that may perhaps interest you?'

Kazia takes the old man's hand, leads him across to the dolls' house. 'Ah . . . I see . . . wonderful! The quality of the painting!'

'It's just a hobby,' Dad explains.

'Jozef loves to make things,' Mum chips in. 'There is nobody better with wood and tin. He is an artist, I've always said so.'

'There's no money in it,' Dad shrugs. 'No future.'

The old man sits down in the corner of our sofa. His eyes are shining, and his cheeks are red and rosy above the bushy beard.

'I think there could be,' he says. 'Mr Mikalski, I have a workshop, a business, just a mile from here. I make rocking horses . . . old-fashioned ones, handcarved, handpainted. Each one is worth over a thousand pounds, some much more, and we have a waiting list of customers from all around the world. I have made a good living for many years.'

Dad frowns. 'Rocking horses . . . yes, I can see that would be a skill. But . . .'

'I'm almost at retirement age,' the old man says. 'I want to go on working, but I can't do as many hours as I used to. I have two young apprentices and, up until last week, a manager who ran the workshop for me. And then, with no warning, my manager left – he met a Scottish woman on an Internet dating site, would you believe, and he's gone to live in Inverness. It took me years to find someone with traditional woodwork skills, toy-making skills. And now he's gone . . .'

Dad's eyes glitter in the half-light. He is listening now, really listening, and Mum takes my hand and wraps an arm round Kazia, and we stand quietly, watching, waiting.

'You are offering me a job?' Dad asks. 'A management job?'

'There would be a trial period, of course,' the old man says. 'But if it works out . . . it's a well-paid position, Mr Mikalski, and one that I think might suit you. Are you interested?'

Mum squeezes my hand very tightly, and the breath catches in my throat.

'Very interested,' Dad says.

So we get what we want for Christmas after all . . . the chance to stay in Liverpool. It's still just a chance, because jobs don't always work out, of course, but it's enough to wipe the sad, grey shadows and worry lines clean off Dad's face.

Mum is so excited she phones Karen and asks if she really meant it, about the cafe job. The answer is yes, and she whirls the three of us round and round the flat, laughing, whooping, crying. We wrap up warm and go out into the swirling snow, to Midnight Mass at St Peter and Paul's. The church is packed. Everyone sings 'Silent Night', and afterwards we see Frankie and her mum in the porch, and Tomasz and Stefan and even Lily Caldwell.

She catches my eye as everyone files out of church, and I remember what Frankie said and can't find it in me to hate her, not any more. At Christmas, like Dad says, you put old grudges behind you. I smile, because it's Christmas, and because we're not going back to Krakow after all, not yet anyway. Lily blinks and drags up a wobbly smile of her own, and wishes me Happy Christmas, which is a miracle in itself.

'We get to stay after all,' Kazia says, as we shiver into pyjamas. 'And Dad will be in charge of Santa's workshop!'

I open my mouth to correct her, but you know what? The guy does look like Santa, and he even works as Santa now and again, and the workshop makes beautiful wooden toys, so . . . well, I guess she has it right, pretty much.

When I wake, the room is pitch dark, and I can hear Kazia's breathing, soft and rhythmic.

I hear a soft, dull thud against the window pane, and I slide out of bed and pull the stringy curtains aside. A snowball slides slowly down the glass, landing in a heap on the outside window sill. The world is bright and clean and perfect, swathed in white, and leaning against the lamp post across the street is a boy with dark braids and slanting cheekbones.

I pull on my boots, wriggle into a jumper and creep out across the living room, past the tree and the glinting szopka castle. I take my coat from the stand, pull on gloves and hat and scarf, run down the stairs and out into the snow.

Dan looks up, his face shining in the lamplight,

and suddenly I'm shy, tongue-tied, nervous. The last time I saw Dan I yelled at him, said stuff I really, really wish I hadn't. And now I can't help wondering if things will ever be the same between us.

'Hey,' Dan says. 'No pink fluffy slippers tonight?'

'No angel wings?' I counter.

'No. I'm gonna be myself from now on, I guess.' He walks towards me, making fresh tracks in the glinting snow. His melted chocolate eyes are sad, and I know that's partly my fault. I want to run into his arms, hold him tight, but I'm scared . . . scared I've spoiled it all.

Then Dan wraps his arms round me, and I can breathe again. 'I'm sorry,' he says into my hair. 'I'm so sorry, Anya.'

'I know,' I tell him. 'Oh, Dan, I'm sorry too!' And that's it, sorted, as simple as that. I don't tell him about what's been happening for my family, how close we came to going back to Krakow . . . not yet. I'll explain all that later. Right now, I just want to enjoy being with Dan, properly, without any of that stuff to complicate things.

We walk to the park. Snow has made the world brand new, covering up the dirt and litter with a thick blanket of white. The park is a magical landscape, familiar but other-worldly, a place where anything seems possible.

'I'm not like my dad,' Dan says quietly.

'I know,' I tell him. 'I was upset, angry – trying to hurt you.'

'It really *didn't* mean anything,' Dan goes on. 'The kiss. Lily jumped me, just about. I thought one friendly dance would be OK, but she had other ideas . . .'

'Lily will always have other ideas, when it comes to you,' I sigh.

'Maybe,' Dan huffs. 'But those are her ideas, Anya, not mine. It lasted about a split second. Then I pulled away, and all I could see was you, running away from me, pushing through the crowd . . .'

'I was angry.'

'I know. I'd have been furious. But, Anya, it's you I like – you I want to be with. You're . . . well, y'know. My girl.'

I know that now. I know it because Dan's hand is tight around mine, and he's here with me in the snow, in the dark, on Christmas morning, and that's the best present I will ever have.

'What did you do, after we argued?' I ask.

Dan sighs. 'I walked for hours, all around town, trying to get things straight in my head. I was hurt and angry – with Lily, for her stupid trick, and with you, for not trusting me. But I felt guilty too, because I knew I kind of deserved it, and I didn't want to be like Dad, I really, really didn't.'

We walk right down to the edge of the lake.

'I got it into my head that I should talk to Dad,'

Dan says. 'I'd messed up with him, messed up with you – and it all got tangled up in my head. I wanted to put at least one thing right, and Dad seemed the easiest option. I went to Lime Street Station, but the last train to Manchester had gone. I found an all-night cafe and sat up drinking coffee and planning what I'd say to him, how I'd make him come back. I sat in the cafe all night and caught the first train to Manchester in the morning. By the time I got there, I had no money left, so I had to walk. It was miles and miles, and I got lost a few times, but in the end I found him . . .'

I think of Karen Carney, sitting at our kitchen table, her face grey with worry. I think of Frankie, Kurt and me, working like crazy at the cafe so we wouldn't have time to think, to let in the fears about what might have happened to Dan.

'We were so worried, Dan,' I tell him. 'So scared.'

'I know,' he says. 'I'm sorry. I wasn't thinking straight. It was only when I saw the police at Dad's that I realized just what I'd done, how worried sick everyone must be.'

He leans down to scoop up a handful of snow, packing it into a snowball. 'Make a snowman with me?' he asks.

The two of us roll the little snowball along the ground, gathering snow, laughing, watching it get bigger and bigger.

'We talked, anyway,' Dan says. 'Dad and me. We talked all afternoon, once the police had gone. About why things went wrong, how he fell for somebody new . . . I understand it better now. He was never going to come back. I was just kidding myself I could fix everything up, turn us back into a happy family again.'

'It's not so simple,' I say.

The snowball is waist high now, and we push it to a halt beside the lake, building it higher and higher.

'Not simple at all,' Dan says. 'I see that now. Dad didn't plan to let us down, didn't plan to fall out of love with Mum. You can't choose who you fall for, can you?'

I bite my lip. 'Suppose not.'

I make a smaller snowball, fixing it on to the body of the snowman while Dan hunts for pebbles and stones for eyes.

'The snow's too thick,' he frowns. 'I can't find anything. Oh, hang on . . .' He finds a half-eaten packet of Rolos in his pocket and presses them into the white snow to make eyes, a smiling mouth, coat buttons.

'I'm still angry at Dad,' Dan sighs. 'It doesn't just go away overnight, but . . . well, he still loves me and Ben and Nate.' Dan takes off his scarf and winds it round the snowman's neck.

'Running away wasn't the answer,' he says. 'You can't run from the truth, can you? Staying put and making the best of what you have is better, right?'

'Right,' I say, thinking of our chance to stay in Liverpool, and how it means settling for something that wasn't quite our dream. It still seems like the right thing to do, though.

'I caused Mum almost as much trouble as Dad did,' Dan reflects. 'Skiving school, getting into trouble. I'm going to change, Anya. Grow up, make a go of things, like you said.'

'I'll help you,' I tell him. 'Promise.'

'It's a deal!'

We give the snowman some branches for arms and stand back, admiring our creation. 'He's cool,' Dan pronounces, forming another snowball, packing it tight.

'Cool, yes,' I agree. 'What's the snowball for?'

Dan's eyes twinkle. 'Can't you guess?'

I run then, floundering through the thick snow, the eerie darkness, skidding and slipping and laughing, but the snowball hits me on the shoulder and I stop, gathering up ammunition of my own. I have more experience of snowball fights than Dan, experience gained from a long childhood of white winters back in Krakow, of snowballs thrown in the school playground, snow wars that could divide a class. I pelt Dan until he's begging for mercy, until he catches me, whirling me round and round in the snow, and kisses me. His caramel skin is icy cold against my cheek, but his lips are warm. The kiss is the way I remember, soft and sweet and lingering, but this time it means a whole lot more. It's a kiss that says we know each other, need each other, believe in each other.

'I don't want to lose you,' he whispers into my hair. 'You're the best thing in my life, Anya, you know that?'

I've never been anybody's best thing before, except maybe Mum and Dad's, and that's a position I have to share with Kazia, of course.

'In my life, you're the best thing too,' I whisper, and I know that it's true.

'Have you ever made a snow angel?' Dan asks.

'Snow . . . angel?'

He lets himself fall backwards into the snow, laughing, lying flat out, his arms windmilling up and down. 'Come on! Try it!'

I flop down beside him, the jolt of cold making me squeal. 'Dan!' I yelp. 'We could freeze to death!' Snow sticks to my pyjama legs, creeps in like an icy finger between my scarf and my collar.

'Fun, though,' Dan tells me. 'No cheating. Now, move your arms up and down . . . push at the snow . . .'

I look up at the sky, streaked now with violet and

gold, and I take a deep breath in and reach for Dan's fingers. They wrap around mine, holding tight.

When we stand up, brushing off the snow, shivering, there in the snow is an impression of two bodies with wings. Snow angels.

Dan looks down at them. 'I'm not an angel,' he says. 'I'm just me, OK?'

'I know.'

'Happy Christmas, Anya . . .'

Snowflakes drift down around us as we walk back towards the flat, hand in hand, our faces turned up to the lightening sky.

That was five months ago, and a whole lot of stuff has changed since then. Dad started work with the Santa Claus guy, managing the rocking-horse workshop, and things went well – really well. He's doing a job he loves, learning fast, expanding the business. Orders are flooding in, and still the waiting list grows.

These days, my dad doesn't look worn out and grey-faced and hopeless. He looks like a man with a dream, a dream that might just come true this time.

Mum started work with Karen at the cafe – they were a great team, but keeping that cafe afloat was tough. All those cupcakes and melt-in-the-mouth meringues, the cream slices and luscious chocolate cakes . . . they tasted good, but they just didn't bring in enough cash.

In April, Karen took the decision to close.

'I'll miss the cafe,' Ringo said, breaking into song again. '*Imagine there's no Heaven . . .*'

We rolled our eyes, laughing, but imagining no Heaven . . . well, it was hard.

The cafe closed, and the builders came, and when it opened up again it was a shop, not a cafe. The kitchen is bigger and there's an office part too, where Mum and Karen run the new website. There are sofas and comfy chairs and a catalogue of beautifully designed cakes for special occasions, so that customers can leaf through and decide which one they want for their wedding or birthday or business function. While they choose, they can drink lattes and eat frosted cupcakes for free, and that usually convinces them that they've come to the right place, so the orders keep on coming.

The shop's called Angel Cake.

'Ever noticed that all the people who hung around this place seemed to get a happy ending?' Dan commented. 'Weird, huh? Think it was something in the cake mix?'

Well, maybe. The Lonely Hearts Club was a success, anyhow. Ringo got his girlfriend, and Frankie's mum her new guy . . . but it wasn't until Angel Cake's big opening party that we worked it out. Ringo's girlfriend *was* Frankie's mum.

Frankie nearly fainted with horror when she saw them walk in together, Ringo in his orange satin coat and Mrs McGee in a lime-green minidress.

Things like that can scar you for life, but Frankie's a tough cookie.

She's used to it now. 'It's like Ringo says,' she told me recently. '*All you need is love . . .*'

Dan got his happy ending too – he went into school on the first day of the January term with Karen in tow, and asked to see Mr Fisher. Dan filled the head teacher in on everything that had happened with his mum and dad and all the reasons he'd been feeling so angry, so close to the edge. 'I'll change,' he told Mr Fisher. 'I promise!'

Well, maybe. Dan has a rebellious streak a mile wide, but he is also stubborn and determined and smart. In three short months he has turned his school career around. Miss Matthews has stopped backing away whenever he comes into a classroom, and that has to be good, right?

Frankie and Kurt are still together. Frankie has got into the whole healthy-eating thing big style, encouraged by Kurt, of course. She is vegetarian now, and more likely to be seen snacking on tofu and beansprout salad than scarfing down a plate of chips.

She's lost some weight, and she looks fantastic.

Kurt's gone full-on goth, and last week had a detention from Mr Fisher for wearing black nail varnish in class. True to his word, he found a new home for Cheesy, somewhere the little rescue-rat is loved and fussed and cared for.

Cheesy lives with Lily Caldwell now.

I know that doesn't sound too promising, but trust me, Lily's changed. She's through with boys, and that includes the scally-gang Dan used to hang out with. 'Boys are rats,' she told us, shooting dark looks at Dan, who never actually noticed most of the time. But then, he never noticed when she was shooting him mushy, slushy looks, either, so maybe that's OK.

Anyhow, it was the 'rats' comment that got Kurt thinking, and Cheesy lives in a state-of-the-art rat mansion now, at Lily's place. She's even stopped smoking, because she says it's bad for Cheesy's health. I know – seriously.

She said I could come and visit Cheesy whenever I wanted. She even smiled when she said it, and last week she sat with Frankie, Kurt, Dan and me at lunch and didn't insult anyone, or flutter her spider's-leg lashes at anyone either. She was OK.

'That's rats for you,' Kurt said wisely. 'They have a civilizing effect on almost everyone. A few more weeks, and Lily will probably be joining the school choir and helping old ladies to cross the road.'

I guess you never know.

*

We're moving, and although I said I never wanted to again, this time I think it might be OK.

We are not going back to Krakow. We're moving to Lark Lane, to the flat above Angel Cake, a flat with three bedrooms and a big living room and a kitchen where the sink doesn't leak and the cupboard doors all work. There are new carpets and clean, pale, painted walls and the radiators are new and efficient, not rusty and rattly.

The flat above the shop has been empty since the end of April, when the last tenants moved out. Karen offered it to us, and Dad started work pretty much right away, painting the walls, putting up shelves. Mum made new curtains for the windows, a rag rug for the fireplace.

It's not exactly like the whitewashed cottage I pictured in my mind, but still, it feels like home.

Dad is still shifting boxes and bin bags, with help from Ben and Nate and Tomasz. Tomasz has a removals business now, but this is one move he isn't charging for.

Kazia and I have the attic bedrooms, up above the main bedroom and the living area. I let Kazia pick first, and I end up with the one at the back, with a soft blue carpet and a pine chest of drawers and a single bed with a bright blue duvet. I put my suitcase down and drift to the window, and my heart flips over.

There's a back garden, a secret hideaway, green

and lush and slightly overgrown. All that time I've spent at the cafe and I never realized . . .

I run down to the living room. 'There's a garden!' I exclaim. 'A proper garden!'

Dad laughs. 'Good surprise, huh? I will grow vegetables and your mother will grow flowers, and all of us will have some green space, somewhere to relax.'

Downstairs, tucked in behind the staircase, I find the back door. I turn the key in the lock, step out on to a crooked gravel path and walk through towering clumps of greenery starred with blue and pink and gold. The spring sun warms my face, and as I look up I see the first swallows of the year swooping around the eaves, whirling and looping through the air like acrobats.

'Swallows!' I breathe.

When I turn back to the house, I see that the back door is painted a glossy red, like in the cottage I once imagined, and an unruly climbing rose is twining its way around the doorframe, its green and white buds still tightly furled, but ready, sometime soon, to open and flower. Dreams have a way of coming true, after all.

Karen and Dan appear in the doorway, carrying wine and lemonade and cake boxes. 'C'mon, Anya!' Dan says. 'Flat-warming! Are you gonna show us around?'

On the path at my feet there is a single white feather, soft enough and pure enough to have fallen from an angel's wing. I pick it up, smiling, and go inside.

Turn the page for a sneak peek
of the first book in

The Chocolate Box Girls

Cathy's *brilliant*, brand-new series . . .

Cherry Crush

It is great to have a dad who believes in you, who backs you up and defends you from mean-faced teachers. It is great to know that Dad thinks I am creative and imaginative, but there is a little voice inside me that wonders if, sometimes, sticking to the truth might just be easier all round.

Stories come easily to me, that's the trouble. A teacher asks me where my history essay is and, right away, a fully formed story pops into my head about how our flat was burgled the night before and my essay was taken away by police detectives as evidence, to be dusted for fingerprints and DNA. I forgot my gym kit, once, and I told the teacher our washing machine had gone wrong, shredding it all into spaghetti-like strips before flooding the kitchen and bringing down the ceiling of the flat below.

It sounds so much better than saying 'I forgot it', so much more interesting and colourful and adventurous. The trouble is, my teachers tend not to agree. They prefer the truth, even if it is dull and grey and boring.

Is it really such a crime, to have a vivid imagination?

'I've explained it all now,' Dad is saying. 'Miss Jardine doesn't think you have settled in too well at Clyde Academy. She says that a fresh start might be for the best.'

❀❀❀❀❀❀❀❀❀❀❀❀❀❀❀❀❀❀❀❀❀❀❀❀❀❀

'I settled in fine!' I say, outraged.

Well, maybe I didn't . . . but I scraped by, didn't I? Miss Jardine has made it all sound so much worse than it really is, so much more of a big deal. And none of this would have happened at all if it hadn't been for Kirsty, of course.

'She deserved it, anyway,' I say. 'Kirsty McRae.'

Dad raises an eyebrow. 'Is this the same Kirsty who came to tea when you were seven, and ate all the Taystee Bars and made you cry?'

'That's her.'

'Well . . . perhaps,' he sighs.

Kirsty's long-ago visit stirred up a whole lot of trouble, but I was grateful to her too, in a funny way. She made me ask questions I'd never even thought of asking before.

I was seven years old, and I'd never wondered where my mum was, or why I looked so different from Dad or from the other kids at school.

'Am I adopted?' I had asked Dad, a few days later. He'd rolled his eyes and folded me in his arms and wiped my tears away, and later he gave me a photograph of my mum, young and beautiful and laughing, her ink-black

❁❁❁❁❁❁❁❁❁❁❁❁❁❁❁❁❁❁❁❁❁❁❁❁

hair blowing back in the breeze on the beach at Largs. I was only seven, but I knew even then that I would look just like her, one day. Dark, almond eyes, high cheekbones, skin the colour of milky coffee.

Her name was Kiko and she was Japanese. I was half-Japanese, and I hadn't even known it.

I never missed my mum until I saw that photograph, I swear. Afterwards, though, she was all I could think about. I got books out of the library about Japan. I drew endless felt-pen sketches of dark-haired ladies in kimonos, twirling parasols, even though in the photo my mum was wearing jeans and a jumper. I would imagine pagodas and cherry blossom and brave samurai warriors.

'Are we really leaving Glasgow?' I ask Dad now.

'We really are,' Dad says. 'No more Miss Jardine. No more Kirsty McRae . . .'

I laugh. We clank Coke cans and drink to the future, then Dad tries to flick the TV over to the football, so we wrestle over the remote control and I manage to grab it and chuck it across the room, where it lands with a 'plop' in the goldfish-bowl, with Rover giving it the evil eye.

✿✿✿✿✿✿✿✿✿✿✿✿✿✿✿✿✿✿✿✿✿✿✿✿

It starts slowly, the packing up. In the first week of the school holidays, I tidy my room and chuck out a lifetime's supply of broken plastic toys, dusty comics and worn-out plimsolls last seen when I was seven. I sort out a bag of book, two bags of board games and fluffy toys and a bin bag of outgrown clothes for the charity shop. Dad adds a few bags of his own to the haul, chucks the whole lot in the back of the little red minivan and takes a trip to the tip, stopping off at the charity shop on the way.

By the time Dad ticks off his last-ever day at the factory, our flat is starting to look eerily bare. Even my treasures are carefully packed into a big McBean's Taystee Bar box – the kimono, the paper parasol, the fan, the photograph of Mum.

It feels weird, disloyal somehow, packing away my special things. Scary.

'A girl needs a mother,' Mrs Mackie, the old lady next door, used to say. 'Paddy does his best, but . . .' Her voice would trail away sadly.

I told Mrs Mackie that some girls could cope just fine without a mum, look at me and Paddy, after all. I don't think she believed me, and she was right. She knew me a

❀❀❀❀❀❀❀❀❀❀❀❀❀❀❀❀❀❀❀❀❀❀❀

whole lot better than I would ever admit. I wish my mum was still around to say and do all the stuff that mums are supposed to do when their daughters hit their teens, of course I do. An old photo is not much use when you want to ask about periods or bras or boys . . . or why you can never seem to hang on to your friends.

Some things you cannot talk to your dad about.

It's not like I have never wondered what it might be like if Dad met someone special. I'd picture someone pretty and cool who would talk to me about girly, growing-up stuff and take me shopping for shoes and dresses, or maybe someone plump and kind, who'd bake apple pies and hug me when I felt sad. I dreamed up a hundred different versions of the woman who might be my new mum, and pretended to Kirsty McRae that they were real.

A mum was what I wanted, more than anything.

I never realized she might come with strings attached.

Dad found Charlotte Tanberry on one of those Internet sites where friends from hundreds of years ago hook up and catch up on what they've been up to. She was an old friend from his art-school days – the days before Mum, before me.

Dad had had big ideas, back then. He wanted to change the world, paint wild, wonderful canvases the size of walls. He has shown me photos of a skinny boy with sticky-up hair and paint-stained fingers, a boy with big dreams.

And Charlotte . . . she'd studied graphic design. Like Dad, she'd never hit the big time – she was divorced and living in Somerset, running her house as a B&B to make ends meet.

Pretty soon, Dad and Charlotte were chatting the whole

❀❀❀❀❀❀❀❀❀❀❀❀❀❀❀❀❀❀❀❀❀❀

time, remembering the old days. Dad was glued to his laptop every evening, flirting and messaging and falling in love.

Charlotte was blonde and pretty, I could see that, but more importantly she looked kind, as if she laughed a lot. She looked like mum material.

'I like her,' I told Dad, and he grinned and said he liked her too. The two of them started meeting up for mushy weekends, sharing hopes and dreams, making plans for the future. I would stay with Mrs Mackie in the flat next door, wishing, hoping, praying things would all work out.

It was a modern romance, an Internet fairy tale.

'Have you ever wondered if there could be more to life than this?' Dad asked, one evening, looking around the dingy flat. 'If you're letting life pass you by?'

I frowned. 'Not really,' I replied.

But things were changing, even though I didn't know it.

Dad worked at McBean's Chocolate Factory because the shift hours fitted perfectly with my school day. I used to think that was cool – I'd seen Johnny Depp in *Charlie and the Chocolate Factory* – but McBean's wasn't much like that,

❀❀❀❀❀❀❀❀❀❀❀❀❀❀❀❀❀❀❀❀❀❀❀

not really. There were no rivers of chocolate, no everlasting gobstoppers. Dad did not get to wear a velvet tailcoat and top hat, just a plastic apron and a hairnet and nasty rubber gloves, and the work was so dull he said it made his brain ache.

One day I came home from school and found him making chocolate truffles at the kitchen table, melting down McBean's Milk Chocolate Bars over a pan of bubbling water on the cooker.

'Don't you get enough of that, at work?' I asked.

'Don't laugh,' he'd answered. 'There's money in chocolate. If an old-fashioned biscuit like the Taystee Bar can sell so well, imagine what you could do at the top end of the market. Handmade, organic truffles, beautifully packaged . . . we could make a fortune!'

I looked at the gloopy mess in the mixing bowl and wasn't quite so sure, but we tried a few, and they tasted a whole lot better than they looked.

The next day, he made another batch, packaged them up in a little card box he'd made and decorated himself, lined with gold tissue paper and tied up with ribbon. He sent them off through the post to Charlotte.

❀❀❀❀❀❀❀❀❀❀❀❀❀❀❀❀❀❀❀❀❀❀❀❀❀

She told him they were fabulous, but Dad said he could do better. He switched from melting down McBean's Milk Chocolate to something more upmarket, and the quality of his kitchen-table truffles began to improve. Some of them were pure brilliant, like the ones with fresh strawberries and cream and the ones with tiny chunks of pineapple and mango.

Charlotte got samples of every batch. It was a long-distance love affair, sweetened by chocolate.

Who could resist?

Charlotte came to Glasgow and the three of us went out on a date, to the park, to the museum, to a Japanese restaurant. Dad wore a new jacket and T-shirt and put gel in his hair to try to tame it. I thought he looked great, my smiley, scruffy, lovely dad, with his rumpled brown hair and laughing blue eyes and his ancient Doc Marten boots that leak in the rain. I guess Charlotte thought so too.

She laughed a lot, and when she couldn't manage the chopsticks at the Japanese restaurant she ended up wearing them in her hair. The three of us stayed up past midnight, squashed on to the sofa drinking mocktails Charlotte had invented out of things like peach juice and

❀❀❀❀❀❀❀❀❀❀❀❀❀❀❀❀❀❀❀❀❀❀❀

Irn-Bru and pineapple slices. The next day, at the railway station, she hugged me tight, told me to look after Paddy and said that she'd miss me, and I was so happy I felt like I could fly.

So what if Dad was in love? I was too.

'How would you feel,' Dad had asked carefully, 'about leaving Glasgow? Going down to England to live with Charlotte? We could help her run the B&B, and actually get this chocolate business off the ground. And . . . Cherry, we could be a proper family again . . .'

How would I feel? Like all my Christmases and birthdays had been rolled into one.

Only now it's actually happening, I'm not so sure.

What if it doesn't work out the way I've imagined? What if playing happy families is a whole lot harder than it looks?

It doesn't take long to pack the flat up, not once Dad is finished at the factory. The stack of boxes and bin bags by the door gets bigger and bigger. Towards the end of the week, Mrs Mackie comes round, armed with furniture polish and dusters and a mop and a bucket filled to the brim with soapy water. She puts us to work dusting and polishing and mopping the flat, from top to bottom.

❀❀❀❀❀❀❀❀❀❀❀❀❀❀❀❀❀❀❀❀❀❀❀❀

'I'll miss you, you know,' she tells us gruffly, as Dad scrubs, scours and bleaches the sink and I polish the taps to a high gleam. 'You were never any trouble, as neighbours.'

'We'll miss you too, Mrs Mackie,' Dad says.

I think of all the times she took me to school because Dad was on early shift, all the times I holed up in her flat eating shortbread biscuits and watching children's TV, waiting for Dad to get home.

Mrs Mackie shakes Dad's hand and presses a warm fifty-pence piece into my palm, and tells me to be a good girl. A sad twist of regret lodges in my chest suddenly, and I want to hug her tight and cry on her shoulder . . . I don't, though. I am trying to be brave. After all, I am getting exactly what I wanted. A mum, a future, the chance to be a family, a chance to be like all the other girls – the Kirsty McRaes of this world. It's just that it feels a whole lot more real, more scary, than I ever imagined . . .

We have been up since six, loading the van, struggling up and down the tenement stairs and out into the lashing rain. Every box, every suitcase and bin bag, is shoe-horned in. Mrs Mackie appears in her nylon housecoat and tartan

✿✿✿✿✿✿✿✿✿✿✿✿✿✿✿✿✿✿✿✿✿✿✿✿✿✿✿

slippers, and hands us a bag of cheese-spread sandwiches cut into triangles and a couple of slices of fruit cake for the journey. My eyes really do mist over then.

We abandon the brown corduroy sofa, post the keys through the letterbox for the landlord, and by nine o'clock we are on our way.

'I won't miss the rain,' Dad says, trying to be chirpy.

But I think it's raining because we are leaving, because it's the end of something, and the city is sad to see us go.

By eleven, we have covered more than a hundred miles and it is still chucking down. The downpour is starting to feel less like a sad farewell and more like a really, really bad omen. What if this whole move south and find-a-new-family adventure turns out to be a disaster?

I huddle in the passenger seat, holding Rover in his glass bowl, the box of treasures at my feet. My cheek rests against the window, and outside the rain slides down the glass like tears.

'This summer . . . we'll try to see it as a trial,' Dad is saying. 'See whether we can make things work. I think we can, but I want you to know that you come first, whatever happens. If you're not happy . . . if you don't settle . . . well,

❀❀❀❀❀❀❀❀❀❀❀❀❀❀❀❀❀❀❀❀❀❀❀

we will think again. You're still my number-one girl, Cherry. You know that.'

'I know,' I say softly, but I'm not sure if I do any more, or how long that might last.

Charlotte Tanberry is cool. She laughs a lot, wears chopsticks in her hair, but . . . there is one tiny problem. Charlotte doesn't need a new family because she already has one . . . four bright, beautiful daughters.

I stare out of the window as the little van heads south, leaving Scotland – and life as I know it – behind.

It stops raining just north of Preston, and the sun comes out and a big, beautiful arc of rainbow shimmers over the motorway. We stop at a service station for coffee and milk-shake, eating the cheese-spread sandwiches sneakily, under the table of the service station cafe.

I fish around in my bag for the letters sent by Charlotte's daughters, Skye, Summer and Coco, to tell me about themselves and make me welcome.

Skye's letter is written on black paper in silver gel pen and sprinkled with tiny silver stars; she tells me all about horo-scopes and history and her addiction to jumble-sale dresses. Very odd. Summer's is written in purple on pale pink paper, and her letter is all about ballet and how she dreams of learning to dance *en pointe* and being a prima ballerina one

❀❀❀❀❀❀❀❀❀❀❀❀❀❀❀❀❀❀❀❀❀❀❀❀

day. The last letter, Coco's, is written in smudgy pencil on a torn bit of paper that looks as though it has fallen in a puddle, or been chewed by a dog, or possibly both. Coco seems to be obsessed with animals and climbing trees, and tells me all about her ambition to have a llama, a donkey and a parrot as pets.

I'm not sure if the letters are comforting, exactly.

Dad has met the girls, of course, a couple of times, on trips down south, but he travelled midweek, using odd days off, and each time I was left in Glasgow with Mrs Mackie. I wish now I'd asked to meet them, once at least.

Coco is the tomboy, he reckons, and Skye and Summer are twins, a year younger than me. There is another sister, Honey, just a few months older than I am. 'Charlotte says that Honey didn't have time to write a letter,' Dad explains. 'She's the eldest, six months older than you . . . she's just finishing Year Nine at the high school. You'll be in the year below her, if everything works out. The younger girls are still at middle school . . . that's the way the system is in Somerset.

'Anyway, Honey's had end-of-term exams to revise for, but I'm sure she's really excited about meeting you. She's very pretty, and clever, and confident . . . . I'm sure you'll be great friends!'

'Right,' I say.

'The English school holidays have only just started,' Dad reminds me. 'So you'll have plenty of time to settle in and get to know the girls before you start school. An extra-long holiday . . . brilliant, huh?'

'Yeah . . . brilliant.'

I bite my lip. Dad doesn't understand, really. I am not good at fitting in, making new friends. I am not pretty, or clever, or confident, and Charlotte's children sound all of those things. Being part of a family is way more complicated than I imagined. I never expected sisters to be a part of the deal. Even their names make them sound arty and bohemian and rock-chick-cool.

I can see that I will be the one misshapen Taystee Bar in a family of perfect chocolate-box girls. Great.

It's hours and hours before we finally turn off the M4 to bump along the quiet Exmoor lanes. I am tired and cramped and nervous, and even Rover is looking slightly carsick.

We drive through the pretty village of Kitnor, with its

✿✿✿✿✿✿✿✿✿✿✿✿✿✿✿✿✿✿✿✿✿✿✿✿✿✿✿

thatched, whitewashed cottages crowded together along the roadside. The sun is still shining, as if it never does anything else in a place like this.

'Almost there,' Dad says, and panic twists inside me. What if everything I ever wanted turns out to be a disappointment, like a Christmas present you've prodded and dreamed about . . . and then when you open it, turns out it is a handknitted jumper, sludge-green and baggy and slightly lopsided?

I have a few jumpers like that, now that I think about it. Dad is a big fan of charity-shop chic. It has taken me forever to work out what suits me, steering away from the baggy jumpers and finding refuge in primary-coloured skinny jeans and tight cartoon-print T-shirts and plastic bangles, all cheap as chips from Primark or New Look. I will never be a girly girl, but I look OK, except on the days I manage to decorate myself with jam stains or toast crumbs, or splatter my Rocket Dogs with mud.

There's a glimpse of the sea, glinting silver, and then we're driving through steep, thickly wooded hillside. There's a wooden sign jutting out from the hedge that says *Tanglewood House B&B*, and Dad turns the van into

❁ ❁

a curving driveway fringed with slender, twisty trees and, finally, we're here.

My first glimpse of Tanglewood House takes my breath away. It's big and old and elegant, made from pale golden stone with little arched windows and swooping slated rooftops. There is even a turret, a slim, rounded tower room way up on the second floor, topped with a pointy roof. This house is huge . . . like a house from a fairy tale, where princesses might live. I don't know if I belong in a place like this.

A handpainted banner flutters in the breeze above us, strung from an upstairs window across to one of the trees . . . *Welcome to Tanglewood, Paddy & Cherry.*

'Look!' Dad grins. 'Isn't that great?'

Suddenly the windscreen vanishes, engulfed by a swirl of rainbow-bright fabric, and Dad brakes sharply in a spray of gravel.

'Coco!' a girl's voice yells out. 'Coco, what are you DOING? You've dropped it!'

Dad gets out of the car, and I follow, still hanging on to Rover's fishbowl. A tawny-haired girl in a floppy, green velvet hat is hanging out of an upstairs window, the banner dangling from her hands down on to the van.

❁❁❁❁❁❁❁❁❁❁❁❁❁❁❁❁❁❁❁❁❁

'Hello, Skye!' Dad grins. 'Did you paint this? It's brilliant!'

'I've only just finished it,' the girl sighs. 'Coco was supposed to be helping me to hang it up, not drop it right on top of you!'

A second figure, a skinny girl of nine or ten, still dressed in untidy school uniform, drops down to the ground from her perch in the branches of a tree just to our right. 'Sorry,' she says, all freckles and cheeky grin. 'The string snapped!' She turns away and sprints off through the garden, shouting, 'They're here! They're here!'

The hat girl has vanished, leaving the dangling banner to slither to the floor in a heap.

'Paddy!'

Out of a side door Charlotte comes running, fair hair flying out behind her, laughing, flinging her arms round Dad. He lifts her up and whirls her round and round, the two of them laughing like there is nobody else in the world, for that moment at least.

It makes my tummy flip over.

The hat girl appears in the doorway, arms folded sternly. She is wearing a faded, trailing dress that looks like it came

❀❀❀❀❀❀❀❀❀❀❀❀❀❀❀❀❀❀❀❀❀❀❀❀❀

from some ancient dressing-up box, and a pair of weird, strappy shoes that look about a hundred years old. I try not to stare.

'Mu-um!' she huffs, and Charlotte pulls away from Dad, laughing, and hugs me tight.

'Cherry!' Her warm hands squeeze mine and her green eyes shine. 'I can't believe you're finally here! I want you to feel that this is your home too . . . I can see you've met Skye already, and Honey, Summer and Coco can't wait to get to know you too! We've planned a little party, in the garden – nothing fancy, just family and a few friends and some of the B&B guests . . .'

She bends down to scoop up the fallen banner. 'Looks like we weren't quite in time with this,' she grins. 'Never mind . . . Paddy, you'll help me hang it down in the garden, won't you? There's a stepladder just there, against the wall. Skye, you and Cherry can check on the last bits of food for me, and bring them down . . . let's get this party moving!'

Dad shrugs, picks up the stepladder and follows Charlotte off down the garden. I am stranded on the gravel, clutching Rover's bowl. Skye takes it from me and turns back into the

❁ ❁

house, with me following. 'We've never had a goldfish,' she says. 'We've got a dog, though, and some ducks . . .'

I step into a warm kitchen that smells of sausages and baking. There's a big kitchen table laden with freshly iced chocolate sponge, trifle, cupcakes and strawberry tarts, and a tatty blue dresser with lots of mismatched china, and a pinboard made of real corks, crammed with postcards and little reminder notes. There is even a photo of me and Dad, taken on Charlotte's weekend in Glasgow, and that makes me smile.

Skye puts Rover's bowl down on the dresser and heads straight for the Aga, a big old-fashioned, cream-coloured range cooker, to haul out trays of little sausages and two golden quiches that smell fantastic.

'Here,' she says, handing me a box of cocktail sticks from the dresser drawer. 'Get the sausages speared up. I'll do some tomato and cheese kebabs, because Coco is going through a vegetarian phase. Are you hungry?'

'Starving,' I say.

'Have a sausage,' Skye says. 'Or a cupcake – I won't tell! I didn't think I wanted another sister, but . . . well, I'm glad you're here!'

❀❀❀❀❀❀❀❀❀❀❀❀❀❀❀❀❀❀❀❀❀❀❀❀

'I'm glad too,' I say, and I'm surprised to find I mean it. 'Everything's just so . . . well, perfect!'

Skye laughs. 'It's definitely not perfect,' she tells me. 'But hey, it won't take you long to work that out! Who needs perfect, anyhow?'

She takes a tub of glacé cherries from the cupboard and sticks a whole bunch of them round the edges of the iced chocolate cake on the table.

'We made this for you, specially . . . it's a Cherry Chocolate Cola Cake. We sort of made it up.'

'Thank you!' I say. 'It sounds . . . um . . . amazing!'

Skye loads the cakes up on to a wide tray while I try to balance plates of sausages, veggie kebabs and quiche on another, wobbling slightly. 'You'll get used to it,' she says. 'We have to help Mum out with the B&B breakfasts, sometimes.'

As I follow Skye out to the back of the house, I notice strings of fairy lights draped through the trees, and the beat of an old Mika song and the smell of woodsmoke drifting up across the sloping lawn. In the distance, I can see a bunch of people crowded together around a bonfire, talking, laughing, eating. If this is a small party, I'd hate to see a big one.

❀❀❀❀❀❀❀❀❀❀❀❀❀❀❀❀❀❀❀❀❀❀❀❀❀

There are trestle tables draped in bright tablecloths, crowded with food and drink, deckchairs and a patchwork of blankets and cushions scattered across the grass, and there's a shaky figure on a stepladder, fixing the welcome banner to a tree branch. Dad.

I am picking my way carefully across the grass, trying to keep the tray level, when through the trees to my right, I catch a glimpse of something amazing. There's a little oasis of trees, and among the trees, in a clearing, stands a beautiful bow-top gypsy caravan. It looks like something from a storybook, all glossy curves and rich red, yellow and green patterning. A red gingham curtain flutters from the tiny open window. Behind it all, I can see the glint of a stream, curving through the long grass like a silver ribbon.

'Who lives there?' I ask Skye.

'In the old caravan? Nobody. We used it as a den sometimes, when we were kids . . .'

She walks on, but I can't move, can't stop staring at the caravan. I remember seeing one down in the Borders, when I was little and we were staying with Dad's old art school friends. The caravan was parked up beside the road while its owners boiled a kettle over a makeshift campfire and

❀❀❀❀❀❀❀❀❀❀❀❀❀❀❀❀❀❀❀❀❀❀❀❀

shared out bread and cheese. They looked tanned and tough and slightly scruffy, and the girl had long raggedy hair threaded through with a million different-coloured ribbons. Nearby, a speckled gypsy horse with feathery feet was tethered, eating grass.

Dad said the caravan belonged to New Age travellers, but that not so very long ago real Roma gypsies had lived in caravans like that. They were adventurers, he said, wild and free and romantic.

I thought that the New Age travellers looked wild and free and romantic too, and I told Mrs Mackie about it, once we were home in Glasgow.

'I wouldn't be surprised if there was a little bit of the gypsy in your family,' she told me. 'Paddy's done his share of adventuring, hasn't he? That gap year, or whatever you call it, after art college. Well, of course, it turned into more than a year . . .'

'That's when he met my mum,' I said. 'Maybe she had a little bit of the gypsy in her, as well?'

Mrs Mackie said that she didn't know about that, but she sang me a sad, old-fashioned song about a girl who ran off with the raggle-taggle gypsies, and I liked that. I used to wonder if my mum had run away with the gypsies too. Why not? It was just as likely as the other stories I imagined.

And now I have walked into a whole new life, a life that seems too good, too perfect to be true. A new mum, a proper house, a bunch of brand-new sisters, a beach . . . and a gypsy caravan in the garden. I can't stop grinning.

It can't get any better than this . . . can it?

the *Cast* and *Crew* of

Angel Cake

Kurt

Likes:
Frankie
beansprouts
Cheesy

Dislikes:
Cruelty
Junk food
Mr Critchley

Frankie

Likes:

goth/punk/emo
black hair dye
sponge pudding
& custard

Dislikes:
rats
beansprouts
Crimplene flares

Dan

Likes:

Anya
Cakes
midnight bike rides
late-night picnics

Dislikes:

School
rules
PSE lessons
betrayal

Anya

Likes:

Dan
angel cake
Swallows
dreaming
Liverpool
Christmas
Snow

Dislikes:

Lily
bullies
rain
Peeling wallpaper

Cheesy

Likes:

Kurt
Cheese
Wardrobes

Dislikes:
Mr Critchley

Six Steps to
ANGEL CAKE HEAVEN

INGREDIENTS ...

2 ¼ cups plain flour
1 ⅓ cups sugar
2 large free-range eggs
3 teaspoons baking powder
½ teaspoon salt
½ cup butter/margarine
1 cup milk
1 teaspoon vanilla essence

CHOCOLATE ICING:
150g butter – softened
250g icing sugar
2 tablespoons cocoa powder
2 teaspoons very hot water
Chocolate buttons or your
  favourite sweets

YOU WILL NEED ...

A cupcake baking tray, a mixing bowl, cupcake paper liners,
a wooden spoon or electric mixer, a spatula and a sieve
(Ask an adult to help you use the whisk, preheat the oven and put the cakes in.)

♥ Preheat your oven to 180°C/350°F/Gas Mark 4.
  Put paper cases in the cupcake tray.

♥ Put the flour, sugar, baking powder and salt into a
  large bowl. Mix well.

♥ Add the butter, milk and vanilla. Beat for 1 minute until
  thick and gooey, and add eggs. Beat for a further 1
  minute on medium speed then 2 minutes on high speed.

♥ Spoon cupcake mix into tray until ½ to ⅔ full and bake
  for 20–25 minutes. Leave to cool on a cooling rack.

♥ For the icing, beat together the butter and icing sugar.
  Mix the cocoa powder and water in a separate bowl.

♥ Add the combined cocoa powder and water to the
  butter and sugar, beat until smooth and creamy then swirl
  over your angel cakes. Decorate with choccy buttons or
  any sweets to make your own delicious angel cake treats.

YUM!

icing
sugar

CREATED BY
Candy Cakes

Cathy's Sticky Caramel Cupcakes

GET YOURSELF:

A cupcake tray and paper cases
1 free-range egg – lightly beaten
40g self-raising flour
125g plain flour
155ml milk
80g golden syrup
145g brown sugar
140g butter
100g dark chocolate

FOR THE TASTY TOPPING:

2 tsp hot water
2 tbsp cocoa powder
250g icing sugar
150g softened butter
Chopped nuts
Chocolate chips

 Preheat the oven to 170°C/340°F/Gas Mark 4 and put the paper cases in the tray.

 Take a small saucepan and add the butter, choccy, sugar, syrup and milk, and stir over a low heat until melted. Leave to cool for 15 minutes.

 Take a bowl and sift the plain flour and self-raising flour into it. Then add this flour to the caramel mix and stir in the egg. Mix until it's just combined.

 Spoon the cupcake mix into the tray in equal amounts and bake for 30 minutes. Leave to cool on a cooling rack.

 For the topping, beat the butter and sugar together. Combine the cocoa powder and water, and add to the buttery mixture. Beat until it's all soft and smooth and swirl over the cupcakes. Add chopped nuts and chocolate chips – now enjoy!

Gingersnap Cookies
(makes 20+)

You will need ...

350g plain flour
175g light brown sugar
2 tablespoons golden syrup
½ teaspoon ground cinnamon

100g butter/marge
1 free-range egg
1½ teaspoons ground ginger
1 teaspoon bicarb of soda

Also, baking trays, large mixing bowl, small bowl, cookie cutters, and icing pens to decorate

(For Shannon-style cookies, add in a surprise sprinkle of chopped apricots/raisins/choc chips/glacé cherries/Smarties/whatever takes your fancy at the 'breadcrumb' stage. Onions are best avoided, though – whatever the story says!!!)

✿ Preheat the oven to 180°C/350°F/Gas Mark 4.
   Grease two baking trays.
✿ Sift the flour into a large mixing bowl, and sift ginger, cinnamon and bicarb of soda on top.
✿ Chop the butter into small pieces and use your fingertips to rub it into the flour until the mixture is like fine breadcrumbs.
✿ Stir in the sugar (and any 'surprise' extras you want to add!).
✿ Beat the egg in a small bowl and combine with the syrup.
✿ Add the egg and syrup mixture to the flour and sugar, and mix together well.
✿ Use your hands to squeeze the mixture into a dough.
✿ Sprinkle some flour on to the worktop and roll the dough until it's half a centimetre thick. Use the cookie cutters to cut star and flower shapes, and place them gently on to the baking trays.
✿ Continue until all the dough is used up, then place trays in the oven and bake for 10–15 minutes until golden brown.
✿ Leave to cool . . . then decorate with icing pens . . . and share with your bffs!

THE REAL-LIFE ANYA

Anya was a girl I met after a high-school event in Liverpool. After the signing, a teacher approached to introduce me to one of her pupils: a tall, pretty and shy Polish girl.

My books were some of the first she had read in English. She had written a short piece describing her first days in the UK, at a different school in the south, and she and the teacher wanted to share this with me. The piece of writing was fab — the grammar wasn't perfect and the spellings weren't all correct, but the feelings jumped off the page. I loved it. Before I left, the teacher asked if I had ever thought of writing about a girl coming to the UK from Poland and I admitted that I hadn't.

I had no plans to write a book like that, but over the next few months I couldn't forget the Polish girl or her piece of writing. Slowly, a story began to form in my mind, and I chose to set it in Liverpool as that was a city I'd lived in and fallen in love with while a student, so I knew it well. I chose the name Anya for my main character . . . later I found out that the original Polish girl's name really WAS Anya!

I did a big book tour for *Angel Cake* and ended up at an amazing signing at the big Waterstone's in Liverpool One . . . after signing for hours, the end of the queue was in sight and a striking tall, shy girl approached me. 'Do you remember me?' she asked. It was the real-life Anya! I was stunned and so, so happy . . . it was so fab to see her, and the perfect end to my tour! Anya later emailed and told me how she was doing . . . she has done her exams and is hoping to study art, but still loves writing as a way of expressing her emotions. And reading, of course! Although she didn't know it at the time, she was a big inspiration to me . . . and the story she inspired has gone on to touch many thousands of readers. Pretty cool, huh?

Cathy Cassidy x

Which Chocolate Box Girl Are You?

Your perfect day would be spent . . .
a) visiting a busy vintage market
b) with your favourite canine companion on a long walk in the countryside
c) curled up on the sofa watching black-and-white movies with
    your boyfriend
d) window-shopping with your BFF
e) sipping frappuccinos in a hip city cafe

Your ideal boy is . . .
a) arty and sensitive
b) boy? No thanks!
c) a good listener . . . and a little bit quirky
d) polite and clever
e) good looking and popular – what other kind of boy is there?

Who's the first person you would tell about your new crush?
a) your sister – she knows everything about you
b) your pet cat . . . animals are great listeners
c) your BFF
d) your mum   she always has the best advice
e) no one. It's best not to trust anyone with a secret

Your favourite subject is . . .
a) history
b) science
c) creative writing
d) French
e) drama

Your school books are . . .
a) covered in paisley-print fabric
b) a bit muddy
c) filled with doodles
d) neat, tidy and full of good grades
e) rarely handed in on time

When you grow up you want to be . . .

a) an interior designer
b) a vet
c) a writer
d) a prima ballerina
e) famous

People always compliment your . . .

a) individuality. If anyone can pull it off you can!
b) caring nature – every creature deserves a bit of love
c) wild imagination . . . although it can get you into trouble sometimes
d) determination. Practice makes perfect
e) strong personality. You never let anyone stand in your way

Mostly As . . . *Skye*

Cool and eclectic, friends love your relaxed boho style and passion for all things quirky.

Mostly Bs . . . *Coco*

A real mother earth, but with your feet firmly on the ground, you're happiest in the great outdoors – accompanied by a whole menagerie of animal companions.

Mostly Cs . . . *Cherry*

'Daydreamer' is your middle name . . . Forever thinking up crazy stories and buzzing with new ideas, you always have an exciting tale to tell – you're allowed a bit of artistic licence, right?

Mostly Ds . . . *Summer*

Passionate and fun, you're determined to make your dreams come true . . . and your family and friends are behind you every step of the way.

Mostly Es . . . *Honey*

Popular, intimidating, lonely . . . everyone has a different idea about the 'real you'. Try opening up a bit more and you'll realize that friends are there to help you along the way.

A gorgeous new series by

Cathy Cassidy

The Chocolate Box GIRLS

Cherry:
Dark almond eyes, skin the colour of milky coffee, wild imagination, feisty, fun . . .

Skye:
Wavy blonde hair, blue eyes, smiley, individual, kind . . .

Summer:
Slim, graceful, pretty, loves to dance, determined, a girl with big dreams . . .

Honey:
Willowy, blonde, beautiful, arty and out of control, a rebel . . .

Coco:
Blue eyes, fair hair, freckles, a tomboy who loves animals and wants to change the world . . .

Each sister has a different story to tell, which will be your favourite?

Random Acts of
Kindness

Copy cool Sam Taylor from *Ginger Snaps* and try a random act of kindness every day. Here are a few to start you off . . .

- ♥ *Wash up* without being asked
- ♥ *Hug* a friend!
- ♥ *Talk* to someone who's feeling lonely or left out
- ♥ *Compliment* a classmate on his/her appearance
- ♥ *Send a card* to your BFF for no reason at all
- ♥ *Carry shopping* for an elderly neighbour
- ♥ *Play* with your little bruv/sister – it's fun!
- ♥ *Smile* – it's free, and it makes everyone feel good. Especially you!

And why not show your *BFFs* how much you care by organizing something that you could do together? The most important thing is spending time with each other and having fun!

- ♥ *Throw a mini party for your best friends* – you could all watch a DVD together, or make your own dream flags to hang in your room. Or maybe you could bake your own Angel Cakes!

- ♥ *Hold a cake sale* – once you've baked your yummy cakes, why not set up a stall to sell them? Maybe you could raise money for a charity that really means something to you.

- ♥ *Invite your friends to a clothes-swapping party* – you might not be in love with that sparkly top any more, but maybe one of your friends would look great in it. And you save money by not having to buy new clothes! Why not make it into a pamper party and spoil each other with some new hair looks?

For more ideas go to www.cathycassidy.com

Best Friends are there for you in the good times and the bad. They can keep a secret and understand the healing power of chocolate.

Best Friends make you laugh and make you happy. They are there when things go wrong, and never expect any thanks.

Best Friends are forever,

Best Friends Rock!

Cathy Cassidy's
MY
BEST FRIEND
Rocks!
Enter at:
www.cathycassidy.com
mizz
AWARD

Is your *Best Friend* one in a million?

Go to *www.cathycassidy.com* to find out how you can show your best friend how much you care

Catch all the latest
news and gossip from

Cathy Cassidy

at

www.cathycassidy.com

- ✦ Sneaky peeks at new titles
- ✦ Details of signings and events near you
- ✦ Audio extracts and interviews with Cathy
- ✦ Post your messages and pictures